T0276701

ADVANCE PRAISE FOR

"Immersive, propulsive, and ı
read this chilling novella is to sit across from your com-
plicity as the weak tea of lean-in feminism and institutional DEI is spilled slowly down your shirt."

> —*Anna Moschovakis, author of* An Earthquake is
> A Shaking of the Surface of the Earth

"Reading poupeh missaghi's courageous *Sound Museum*
is an astonishing experience of profound significance. It
is magnificent."

> —*Rikki Ducornet, author of* The Plotinus

"In a furious mixtape of feminist theory and scholarship
on torture, missaghi constructs a universe beyond clearly
recognizable sides of good and evil. *Sound Museum* turns
the mirror back toward its readers, who, unbeknownst
to themselves, have entered the Sound Museum and
may never leave again."

> —*Yanara Friedland, author of* Groundswell

"To read *Sound Museum* is to watch *The Zone of Interest*
fall into gentle banter with *Tár* on an elevator, bringing us so close to the mouth of evil that we can feel her
breath. I left this book so unsure how to define character
or cruelty, I could barely remember how to walk across
the room."

> —*Aisha Sabatini Sloan, author of* Borealis

"Ignoring the rules of political correctness, poupeh missaghi confronts horror and violence in a direct way, generating an uncomfortable but necessary book that stands in the middle of the unacceptable to intelligently question the forms that atrocity takes and the double standard and Western hypocrisy towards these practices."

—*Carlos Soto-Román, author of*
Alternative Set of Procedures

# SOUND
# MUSEUM

# SOUND
# MUSEUM

## A THEORY FICTION

## poupeh missaghi

**COFFEE HOUSE PRESS**

Minneapolis

2024

Coffee House Press books are available to the trade through our
primary distributor, Consortium Book Sales & Distribution,
cbsd.com or (800) 283-3572. For personal orders, catalogs, or
other information, write to info@coffeehousepress.org.

Coffee House Press is a nonprofit literary publishing house.
Support from private foundations, corporate giving programs,
government programs, and generous individuals helps make
the publication of our books possible. We gratefully acknowledge
their support in detail in the back of this book.

LIBRARY OF CONGRESS CATALOGING-IN-PUBLICATION DATA

Names: Missaghi, Poupeh, author.
Title: Sound museum : a theory fiction / Poupeh Missaghi.
Description: Minneapolis : Coffee House Press, 2024.
Identifiers: LCCN 2024009412 (print) | LCCN 2024009413
   (ebook) | ISBN 9781566896993 (paperback) | ISBN
   9781566897006 (e-book)
Subjects: LCGFT: Novellas.
Classification: LCC PS3613.I84475 S68 2024 (print) | LCC
   PS3613.I84475 (ebook) | DDC 813/.6—dc23/eng/20240304
LC record available at https://lccn.loc.gov/2024009412
LC ebook record available at https://lccn.loc.gov/2024009413

PRINTED IN THE UNITED STATES OF AMERICA

31 30 29 28 27 26 25 24          1 2 3 4 5 6 7 8

The NVLA series is an artistic playground where authors challenge and broaden the outer edges of storytelling. Each novella illuminates the capacious and often overlooked space of possibilities between short stories and novels. Unified by Sarah Evenson's bold and expressive series design, NVLA places works as compact as they are complex in conversation to demonstrate the infinite potential of the form.

*for Armin*

"As if I were being warned a few years in advance or a few centuries too late about . . . the double nature of silence, and the collective catastrophe of which improbable sounds are often harbingers. Improbable sounds and clouds."

—Amulet, *Roberto Bolaño*
*(translated by Chris Andrews)*


« سقوط ما مصیبته / مرگ صدا مصیبته / مصیبته، حقیقته / حقیقته، حقیقته »
آهنگ «سقوط» داریوش اقبالی، ترانه‌سرا شهیار قنبری

"Our fall is a disaster / The death of sound is a disaster / A disaster, a truth / A truth, a truth."

—*"The Fall," a song by Dariush Eghbali,*
*lyrics by Shahyar Ghanbari*

# SOUND
# MUSEUM

**I want to start** by welcoming you to the Sound Museum. I hope the long flights were not too taxing and that your stay at the hotel has been restful so far. And I hope you are aware of what a unique opportunity we're offering you today: you are a select group of foreign journalists chosen after much scrutiny and the first in the world to receive a tour of our truly exceptional establishment. I want to be conscious of your time and will get directly to the remarks I've prepared, accompanied with some slides so you can better follow, to give you some context about our museum before we head into the main wing and you can experience everything for yourselves. How does that sound? Wonderful. I'm glad to hear it. So let's begin with the basics. I really value transparency, unlike many of my colleagues, especially and I'm sure this won't surprise you—the males. I came to realize, during my time as an interrogator and torturer, that our government was not doing a good job maintaining an archive of its achievements. I'm proud of our system, mind you, but that pride has nothing to do with the bureaucracy, or the day-to-day, or the documentation or lack thereof; it's all about the ideology, and even more than that, to be honest, about the spirit of power and control, the thirst for it feeding everything. And who wouldn't feel that way, especially as a woman in a patriarchal system, right? I did my best, in my later years, as a senior member, to shift the gender balance of our workforce, recruiting and training more women. I have many success stories, especially ones about using women for interrogating male prisoners, who are often so full of themselves that they never suspect a woman might be manipulating their male privilege for her own ends, which are, in this case, one and the same with the ends of our system—for example, making them confess to what she needs, giving away some secrets or seemingly trivial information that she can later make good use of. Maybe I'll tell you more about those achievements later, but for now, back to the main point. Unlike many dictatorial and totalitarian regimes, historically and across the globe, ours has not done a satisfactory job of documenting and archiving our interrogation and torture methods. What a loss, really. We've been doing such great work, for so many years, and people on both sides of the line would agree with that, those of us within the administration and those upon whom the techniques have been used. I'm sure many would testify to that if needed, or I guess I should say, if allowed. I began to notice at some point that even though most administrators and directors shared the goal of continually honing their techniques to better serve the system, we ended up doing lots of trial and error, repeating our past methods because of this lack of systematic, scientific passing on of knowledge among ourselves. So I began taking notes after my own sessions, observing sessions led by the younger team members I supervised, and talking to colleagues during our breaks or our rare shared meals or on outings for covert side projects—only those colleagues, of course, who didn't mind sharing their knowledge. Yes, bragging was something they all did, but really looking at what they were doing to understand patterns and trends or being willing to share their experiences in order to teach someone else something—no, that didn't happen, at least not from what I saw. I wonder whether that, too, is in some way related to gender—male superiors not wanting women to know their secrets for success—but then again, I've seen enough of that kind of guardedness within all-male groups as well, so I'm not sure. Anyway, I did talk to those who were willing to be more observant and then pass on small bits and pieces of their knowledge. Torture scholar Darius Rejali, a leading figure in the field, whom I'll refer to often throughout this presentation, along with his book *Torture and Democracy,* confirms that interrogators do "not give away their trade secrets to their rival interrogators." That strikes me as so patriarchal. Because for me, from the very beginning, the aim was not just my success, or that of any one individual, but rather the success of the collective. Many others say this too, but fail to implement it in reality. One of the key goals of this project is to change that mindset of secrecy. We need to become different human beings, with different priorities, if we are to succeed and sustain ourselves. We need to work for the good of the whole, for the collective, rather than fall into the trap of Western individualism. In the course of our history, we have learned, and continue to learn, from our colleagues around the world, though I'm aware that when it comes to torture, each country, era, situation, and even type of prisoner demands its own set of rules and regulations. But still, we all learn from one another. We're in the age of globalization, after all, though I think with regard to torture, we've always been globalized, according to what I've read over years of work on this project. As my interest grew, following my initial observations, I realized we needed to create a museum, a kind of archive, a learning center. And I made it my personal mission to make it happen. I'll tell you later how fucking hard it was to persuade my superiors, all with their fucking male egos, that I, whom they respected for my innovative methods and high success rates, could be the one in charge of this task force, but eventually, I did. A budget was set aside—a small one, in the beginning—and they allowed me to work as a one-woman team only, observing and taking notes. After a while, I found within me a growing curiosity to learn about the history of the field and the theories behind what I had practiced and seen others practice for so many years, to be able to critically think about the choices we were making in order to refine them. I think in part it had to do with the desire, integral to this project, to change the widely held stereotype that we, the torturers, interrogators, and prison staff in general, are just the practical hands of greater minds and not necessarily intelligent ourselves. Despite scholarship to the contrary, the public still tends to take us for imbeciles who just follow orders, for dogmatic people who follow our Supreme Leader with faith as unshakable as that in God—they see no agency in us. We see this to an even higher degree when it comes to our female officers, unfortunately. I've heard people bad-mouthing every woman who wears the black veil, or any outfit that's more conservative, believing that all of us are either close-minded or victims, that we got our positions just because of religious or ideological leanings, not because we're educated, sophisticated, skilled human beings who've made choices and are very good at what we do. These kinds of perspectives, which make caricatures of us, are often far from true, and to be honest, they reveal more about the limited viewpoints of those who hold them than they do about us torturers. I want to make a comparison here to clarify things a bit. Think about those who work in banks and financial institutions, especially in your own countries, where banks hold so much evil power over the rest of society. Are you quick to tag everyone who works for these institutions and dreams of climbing the ladder an idiot? Of course not. You can't dismiss the complex role people's individual personalities play in their career choices, or even in their finding themselves in certain positions and deciding to continue on. That's why, in addition to building the museum, we've made sure to document our entire process. The related materials are on display in our archives wing and will later appear in a book which will also include a transcript of my talk today. The goal has been not just to make the institute more comprehensive and multifaceted and thus more engaging for viewers, but also, for our own sake, to reclaim our agency, our knowledge, our intelligence, and our capabilities as individuals who, like many others in various professions, come together as a team to achieve a shared set of goals they either believe in or find beneficial for one reason or another. I know Hannah Arendt says the main reason many people serving in ruling systems like ours—which she considers totalitarian, though I strongly beg to differ—continue to do what they do is not because of their complexity or their belief in the work but rather because after a certain point, the price of leaving the system becomes much greater than that of staying within it. But that can be said of people in any system or group. Think about yourselves. What would be the price of stepping outside your capitalist system? Outside your patriarchal institutions? What about the price of disobeying your editors' demands? All those decisions would carry a price, would take much courage. And meanwhile, less abstractly, how does Arendt or anyone else expect these individuals to earn a living? Standing outside the system is impossible if you care about your livelihood and flourishing. So Arendt's argument, though compelling, does not really reveal much about our particular choices, the inner workings of our system. You know, actually, Darius Rejali, who unfortunately lives in the US, siding with our enemy, did an interview, I believe with the podcast *On Being,* and spoke about meeting, in his younger years, in the US, one of his distant Iranian relatives, who had been high up in the detestable ex-king's intelligence service and was after our blessed Islamic Revolution of 1979 living in exile. Rejali said how surprised he was that the guy was so well-versed in the arts and philosophy, highly educated, sophisticated, really just a regular person. What did he expect? Why do people imagine that we're not smart? Don't they know how much mental pressure and subtle decision-making each and every interrogation and torture session requires? It really surprises me, the things people assume. I guess it's a general problem, each group of people imagining they're the only smart ones, the only ones who really understand the world we live in, our humanness. Changing this mindset in our visitors, including among your esteemed group, is one thing we hope to do. The further I took my research, the more I realized how we have used the knowledge of other professionals, from those in various medical fields to psychologists and psychoanalysts, from tech geniuses to factory managers to those who are running whole industries, from military personnel to more traditional detectives, from novelists and artists to even parents, if you can believe it, just to give a few examples, to aid us in our work. I was also gradually getting into the philosophy behind our work, wanting to provide a larger contextual framework or even a critical manual for our profession, one feared but also fantasized by many people. As a result, I decided I needed to put together a research group, even if only a small one, to help me create an archive and a research foundation. My project was getting bigger and bigger every day. I knew that, even as smart and capable as I was, I wouldn't be able to bring my vision for the museum to life without the help of a capable, trustworthy team that would also keep the project confidential while underway, especially in the early stages. That was important, because I didn't want any attention we hadn't asked for, and I also didn't want to set expectations we couldn't meet. Most of my male colleagues were too shortsighted to understand long-term dreams like mine as worthy of spending time and resources on. They couldn't absorb how this accomplishment would shape-shift the field of our work forever and leave something invaluable behind for future generations. They were always going on about immediate results, quick attention, return on investment. So we feared that if they learned about the project in its early phases, they would interfere to our disadvantage. More importantly, I also wanted to make sure that no one, especially not external enemy forces, could steal our vision and beat us to it by opening a similar center first, taking all the credit for this unique offering to the world. And finally, our secrecy was a marketing strategy: we were building up curiosity. All this was key while we were hard at work on this project, because it is truly unique and important, not only for me on a personal level but also in a national way. And this doesn't in any way contradict the globalization I mentioned earlier.

Even in the age of interconnectedness, we still need to hold on to our national glory and make sure foreign forces are aware of our achievements—in all fields, but mainly in this one. For all these reasons, it took a long time and a lot of discernment to find the reliable forces I needed, but today, I'm very proud of the all-female team I've put together and what we've achieved. This center is going to change the way things are done in our police force and prison system, I assure you. And I want my entire team to get credit. The original idea for the museum—of course, I'm more than happy to claim that. Now, what I noticed while observing my own sessions and those of my supervisees was that we all paid attention mainly to visual cues. Most of my colleagues believed that to properly document our sessions, we needed to take pictures and videos, which is of course much easier these days because we always carry our phones, many of us at least two of them: one for our personal lives, our family, and the other for our professional lives, which, for a large percentage of us, entail aliases we have built our reputations with. Besides images, the other thing that seemed to matter to most of my colleagues was content, what was drawn out of the prisoner, even though the information they provided, I should clarify, didn't matter most of the time. Within our intelligence agency, unlike many others, where getting information about the prisoner or the people they know really matters, we only sometimes torture so that prisoners will confess urgent items or rat out others. Because of our highly successful surveillance system, all that is beside the point. We mainly interrogate to put on a display of power, to show the prisoner and their larger circle, whether that's family or friends or colleagues, that we can do as we please, to send them a message, to make clear that we have full control over not only their bodies but also their internal states, emotional and psychological, which—you wouldn't disagree with me, I'm sure— is an amazing, intoxicating feeling. As I was explaining, what I noticed was that most often my team members would point out things they would see, like the lighting of the room, whether the prisoner was sitting or standing, the traces we left on their skin or skull, their body language, how they shifted and stirred with our use of different kinds of instruments—stuff like that. But the more I observed and jotted down such information, the more dissatisfied I was. I began to feel there was something missing. I agreed that visual documentation was important, but somehow it didn't get to the heart of the matter, achieve the effect I was hoping my dream museum would have, a corporeal multilayered one, one that pollutes not just the visitors' memories but also their imaginations. I kept thinking about the ways we've often presented our field to the public and how they often remember medieval torture devices, which are kept in museums around the world, images of which also abound on the internet, or how they've heard about modern interrogation techniques, interestingly in the context of the American achievements on the ground at the Abu Ghraib prison. The anecdotes most frequently focus on the goals of the interrogation and torture programs, on our lives, our mentalities, our agendas, personal and professional; in short, they have us, the torturers and the interrogators, as the subject, the focus, which, just to clarify, I'm not against at all. What I'm saying is, that's not what I was interested in, not for our museum. It was key for the research side of things, sure, but for the museum, I wanted to explore and present other layers of our work. There's another way too that the general public often hears about torture, and that's through narratives offered by prisoners sharing their memories of detainment and interrogation, how they broke down or how they survived. Again, I see why such stories are important, even for us, in the sense that they confirm our power, our unique ways of handling things. I asked my team to collect all types of survivors' memoirs alongside the technical information—the instruments and methods we've been using—which are now presented in our archives. Besides these aspects, as I was explaining, I wanted to make sure we had detailed documentation of the process behind building this museum, where it began, the stages it went through, and how it came to fruition. I wanted the project to be not only informative but also creative, so that people could reimagine our relationship to the industry, or rather, as I like to say, to the arts and crafts of our esteemed profession. One day, I was looking at the artwork of an exiled Iranian artist, Siah Armajani, who I think passed away just recently, and I came upon a piece called *Sound Towers*. Let me bring up the slide so we can look at it together. It might not look like anything special, just a few cylindrical towers next to one another, bracketed by two more rectangular structures, but the concept and the title stayed with me, for whatever reason. Isn't it strange how we find inspiration in such odd places? How our innovations rely not only on a combination of intuitive decisions, organized research, and the systems we benefit from but also on keeping ourselves open to synchronicities, to what the world puts in front of us? Armajani's lithograph provides a frontal and rear view of these towers, with some mathematical, geometrical formulas and numbers beneath them. At the time, I was already a few months into my preliminary research, but *Sound Towers* completely upended my previous plan. The caption of the lithograph, as you might be able to read in the slide, says "Sound is generated by the movement of air in the hollow towers," followed by the formulas. That's it, but the attention Armajani was giving sound in the architectural artwork suddenly made me pause and become obsessed with sound from then on. Later, I read in an online source that Armajani was playing with the concept of interweaving moments of silence and sound; the source didn't say much more, and honestly it didn't matter. What mattered was that I was given this new incredible vision for my project of a lifetime, a vision I would not have arrived at without that artist's work. As the Persian idiom goes, "Az to harekat, az khoda barekat," which roughly translates to "You make a move, and God offers you the blessing." What matters is that the heavens offered me their gift on that day. That piece of art shifted the way I went into interrogation sessions from then on. I began to develop an idea of focusing more and more on sound. After all, isn't sound the main premise of interrogation? Where would we be without sound? Isn't the language a prisoner utters or withholds within their throat at the core of our sessions? Without the person's voice, and the role it plays, whether through presence or absence, our work would lose all meaning. So why not just focus on that? Why not have our visitors interact with our work, be inspired by it or terrified by it, through a new medium: sound? Furthermore, I was not primarily interested in *what* was being said, but instead in *how* it was being said or not said, in the interrogation's effect on the prisoner's body, and the oral expressions of that effect. Have you heard about those restaurants where you eat in total darkness? I know, one of those first-world, bourgeois offerings, right? But interesting nonetheless, and as I said earlier, I'm all for taking inspiration from anything, anywhere. The idea of the restaurant is that it rids you of sensory pollution so you can focus only on the taste of your food, evading the rest of your senses and the drama around presentation, restaurant ambience, everything else. In this case, I wanted our visitors not to be distracted by other aspects of an interrogation session, to hear only the sounds uttered by the prisoners, to hold them in their bodies and have them remain there. To clarify, sound is of two different natures. One is the kind that's devoid of language, that is uttered by the body of its own volition, a reaction, which, if you'll excuse my directness, includes the sounds emitted during sexual activity. The other is the sound that carries language with it, drawing our attention because it's saying something, and this one in itself has two different layers as well: the pure acoustic quality of what is being uttered, and the language, by which I mean, the meaning being carried by the sound. Over the course of our experiments with these various types of sound recordings, my team and I decided to curate them by focusing first and foremost on their nonlinguistic elements, because it's on that level that we can prove, without directly telling the visitors, without them even realizing consciously, that we have succeeded in pushing the human beyond what makes them human: the capability to produce language and to express meaning through language. This holds true both during the interrogation and torture and afterward—that is, of course, in the case that the prisoners are released. You're probably aware that many philosophers and scholars have discussed these issues, not necessarily in the context of interrogation, but in similar cases of trauma, especially in relation to the aftermath of Auschwitz. How in the face of extreme horrors, language begins to fail and we, humans, lose our ability for expression, for meaning. If you're interested in learning more about that, I would suggest you start with Maurice Blanchot or Primo Levi, and if you need more information, my team here would be more than happy to guide you toward other resources available at the center's library. Anyway, focusing on the nonlinguistic elements made sense because we also had some concerns with the meaningful, linguistic aspects of the prisoners' voices. Firstly, in our day and age, we're faced with an overabundance of information and are obsessed with the nature of that information, whether it's fact or fiction, true or false. What is the term used in English? Right, "fake news." My thinking was, and our yearslong work on the museum has underlined this further, that by withholding language-based audio that contain information, such as who the prisoner is or why they are imprisoned, and who we are and what we do, we could create a deeper, more embodied relationship between the listener and the sound. They wouldn't listen for semantic meaning in the voice of the interrogator and torturer on the one hand and the prisoner on the other; they would instead have only the pure sounds to hold onto. The second problem with using sound that carries language was the barrier it would create. If we focused only on the content, our audience would be limited to those speaking Persian, and those not speaking the language, including you, would be left out unless given indirect access by translators and interpreters. That approach would introduce another round of problems: we'd need to find reliable translators who would then have to work continuously as new recordings rolled in. Even if we resolved that problem, let's say by using captions, or worse, by dubbing, the visitors would have lost touch with the original voice and all that it carries within it, and their exposure, as a result, would be partial, if not disrupted. This would create an experience similar to watching a foreign film, which many people complain is not emotionally the same as watching and understanding films in their original languages. Or think about artwork that uses words in languages you can't understand, like calligraphy artwork, or what we literally call "calligraphy paintings," in which the words become mere decoration and you lose many layers of meaning. Our aim, thus, became to create our own Sound Towers, though not too similar to those by Armajani, and I'll tell you why. I loved his concept, but I was hoping for a less phallic architectural imagining, for spatial possibilities that would be more feminine, open, and inviting. This might surprise you, especially considering the nature of torture and the whole prison system, as well as our government and yours. They are all about erecting themselves and keeping themselves erect, about penetration and intrusion, about taking space, rather than about holding space and welcoming and embracing and nurturing. Perhaps a phallic structure would have been more suitable, but I was of the belief that aiming for a design that defamiliarized the concepts at hand, one in conflict with expectations regarding a space in which torture is carried out or commemorated, would allow us to pull people in without them even realizing it. Our idea was to invite our visitors into a comforting space and then expose them to various discomforting sounds projected into that space. More on the architectural features later, once we're in the exhibition hall. Back to our preference for using sounds—I want to point to a line of poetry by a famous late Iranian poet, a woman whose poems remain noteworthy in our literary history for their bravery and intimacy, poems we largely disapprove of for these very reasons. We also condemn her behavior and lifestyle, but God rightfully punished her for her wrongdoings by taking her life when she was quite young. You might have heard her name, Forough Farrokhzad. Anyway, the particular line of hers I have in mind has been translated, let me tell you the name of the translator, Elizabeth T. Gray, Jr., to "The sound, the sound, the sound, it's only the sound that remains." The repetition is hers. It's perfect for our mission, right? I know. I had the same reaction when I first made the connection. So we decided to engrave it on a plaque at the entrance to the museum—I don't know if you noticed it on your way in. I won't say I totally agree with her; I mean, logically, it doesn't make sense, because yes, you can record a voice, but you can also take pictures and videos of a person, and those can remain after they're gone as well. Perhaps she was being metaphorical. I don't remember the whole poem, and I know at some point I asked the team to double-check it to see what the context for that line was, but I don't remember the details now. What matters is that the line provides perfect welcoming words for our center. I've heard people use the line often when referring to singers, their voices remaining after their deaths through their recorded songs. For some reason, the first person who comes to mind when I think of this idea, of only the voice remaining, is the legendary Iranian diva Hayedeh. Her voice still gives me goose bumps, all these years after her death, even though we don't approve of the way she lived her life or of the choices she made as a woman or of her singing, sharing her sacred voice with just anyone in all kinds of places. The line also reminds me of an interesting piece I once saw at an exhibition in New York, during one of my research trips. It was at MoMA, though not the main building, but the other one, outside Manhattan, which combines an older building and a new cement construction, and when I visited, there was also a dome-like tent set up in the garden space at the entrance. I didn't go inside the tent, but I found the mixture of various architectural identities charming, the soft and the hard, the warm and the cold, the resulting diversity and fluidity, allowing the eyes to feast on different tastes. So that was another concept I brought to our team of architects and designers later on. I also liked the spaces off to the right of the entrance; they were open-air, but to me they had a prisonlike quality to them, perhaps because of their rectangular layout and concrete material, very simple and cold. But I digress. The exhibition I went to see was about two Iraq wars, one the invasion of Kuwait by Iraq, and the other the invasion of Iraq by the US following 9/11, which revolutionized modern torture techniques. One of the installations, in a room of its own, was dedicated to the use of music as an instrument of torture by us forces. Music— who would have imagined? Excruciating heavy metal was blasting through the loudspeakers while notes about the use of music by the us military to torture Muslim detainees were projected on the screen; the slides were in alternating colors, red and blue, which always, even in that context, remind me of the colors of the two most famous Iranian football clubs, or soccer clubs, as the Americans call them. The installation was by Tony Cokes, an American artist, and it was called *Evil* something. I remember two particular phrases from the slides, "futility music," which highlighted the futility of the detainees' situation, and "cultural music," which was used as an incentive for the detainees. Oh, and there was one other quote I remember: "Disco isn't dead. It has gone to war." Which is cheesy, wouldn't you agree? Anyhow, later I had my team do some more research, and they found that the quotes came from an article called "Disco Inferno" in *The Nation* by a scholar named Moustafa Bayoumi. Even for me, just standing in that room for a short while to read all the slides, the music quickly grew quite disturbing. We have forever been warning our people, especially our youth, about the way American culture and entertainment can be used as weapons; we've always known the West, especially the us, intentionally uses their culture to attract our youth toward their evil ways of life and away from the virtuous teachings of our prophets and leaders, robbing them of their identity and their innocence. I don't want to give a lecture on the dangers of what our Supreme Leader has rightfully called a "soft war," a war our smartest minds have been fighting against in full force for many years, a war that, with the expansion of the internet and social media, has unfortunately become more and more complex these days. The Americans themselves know how harmful and disturbing their cultural products are, so harmful that they can use them even to torture their Muslim detainees in procedures they call "torture lite." Such arrogance in this phrasing! Besides the content and type of music, what makes the method effective is the sheer volume and duration of the music playing on loop. That art installation signaled yet another intersection between sound and torture, and it gave me other interesting ideas, not just about our museum, but rather about how we, too, could experiment with implementing music as a new form of torture. We, too, could begin to use loud music, American music. Not because the people in our prisons necessarily find that music alien or disturbing; no, actually, the exact opposite. If the soft war has already exposed our nation to American culture, and I hardly wish to acknowledge this, but if it has already been successful to a certain degree, then that means people actually connect to it and like it, especially our youth and women, whom I'm so ashamed of, whom we are bringing in more and more of these days, because they've become very good puppets in the hands of our enemies and selling themselves short. So what we aim to do is to completely upend that positive relationship. In our own culture, we've already had lots of success using songs and lamentations to achieve our ideological goals; for example, we used dramatic and epic music to recruit soldiers for our "Holy Defense" or the "Imposed War," terms for the war forced upon us by Iraq, which, mind you, was backed by your governments for many years until Saddam Hussein stopped serving their agendas in the region. Anyway, maybe you've heard the name of a singer of ours, Sadegh Ahangaran, whose emotional, heart-wrenching songs served as influential marches, preparing our soldiers for battle and martyrdom. Another indispensable voice in our battle against Iraq was that of Gholam Koveitipour, who was more of a singer of elegies, though one of my colleagues once noted that he preferred to be described as a singer of epic songs; either way, his songs express the loss of loved ones during the war so painfully and beautifully that they still make me cry all these years later. I don't think I realized, during my younger years, the extent of the power those two voices held, but having now been involved in sound studies for our project for several years, I can say without hesitation that they were key to our efforts to defend the soil of our country against an invading enemy that had all the powers of the world supporting it. We've also long been aware of the power of sound in our religious mourning ceremonies, from the beating of the drums and the rozeh singing—which, for those of you who don't know, is a kind of lamentation performed by clerics for our dead sacred religious figures and almost always brings listeners to tears—to the rhythmic sounds made when our men hit themselves on their shoulders with chains or on their chests with their hands. Sound has always both served us and worked against us. You know, even the monarchy ruling the country before us was in its own way aware of the power of sound and, for that reason, couldn't tolerate the voices of some singers, such as Dariush. The man has been living in exile since we came to power and is unfortunately one of our most outspoken opponents and human rights advocates; with that velvety voice of his, he once opposed the previous regime and now opposes us. I don't understand how some artists, and you see this with some intellectuals as well, can be against both the monarchy and us, against any system of power that has come and gone in this country. Anyway, here's what I'm thinking we can do with music: if we blast American music loud and long in the prison cells, especially in solitary confinement, or even just as background music on repeat for days on end, similar to what our American counterparts have done with their "discos," then we'll be able to make the prisoners confess to whatever we desire just so the music will stop. As an added benefit, this strategy will also make the prisoners hate the music so much that they'll never be able to listen to it again when they leave the prison, since they'll associate the songs with their prison experience. You see what I'm proposing? This gives us wins on several fronts: on the one hand, we'll get immediate results, confessions to be used however we like. Of course, we could achieve these using other methods as well, but the more diverse the measures at our disposal, the better. On the other hand, we'll be able to make the prisoners hate whatever music we expose them to, which they might have once liked, and this in turn will hamper our Western enemies' soft culture wars and limit their ability to infect our youth's minds and tastes. We need only to be careful about the type of music we choose for this purpose, because music can provoke things beyond irritation or disturbance in the prisoner. I don't know if you ever read the memoir *Then They Came for Me.* I haven't myself, but we included it among the books my research team had to study, and it has now been added to the museum archive. I did, however, read an article published by the author, the journalist Maziar Bahari, after he was released from our prison and left the country, preceding the book's publication. The article was published in *Newsweek,* the journal he was on assignment for when we arrested him in Tehran. Anyhow, in that article, he notes that the music of Leonard Cohen helped him survive his solitary confinement. A movie was also made from his memoir, which I did watch. I think it was called *Rosewater,* and there's a very melodramatic scene in which Bahari, or I guess I should say the actor playing him, is remembering Cohen's music, dancing to it in his prison cell. It's interesting that the song Bahari mentioned in his article was

"Hey, That's No Way to Say Goodbye," but the one used in the film is "Dance Me to the End of Love." I guess that second song creates a more dramatic mood for the director to work with. But my point is, if we do, for example, play Mr. Cohen's music for prisoners, it might actually have a soothing effect instead of the disturbing one we're hoping for. You see what I mean? This all is very complicated. Choosing songs they like might not necessarily lead to a change of heart, but might have soothing effects, so we need to monitor the circumstances closely throughout the use of this method. It might also be worthwhile to carry out some experiments and torture using different types of Persian music, the legal songs distributed inside the country versus the ones produced outside Iran, as well as pop songs versus classical and traditional Persian music. My initial thought is that we'd have more luck with songs that are devoid of true musical value, for example, the horrible new pop songs that abound, especially the ones produced in Los Angeles, or music that appeals to only certain audiences, like heavy metal or rap. We have to do more in-depth research here, and consult with trusted musicologists, who will help us make informed decisions before we begin adapting these methods. It would be interesting to consider compiling personalized torture music playlists based on each inmate's likes and dislikes, which we can easily determine in the early stages of the interrogation by using a questionnaire; by gaining access to their music apps, such as Spotify or

SoundCloud, their downloads from torrent sites, or whatever it is the kids are using now; by browsing through the folders on their personal laptops, which we seize; or even by obtaining that information from our people, who've been surveilling them long before they are arrested and brought in. We can even benefit from the algorithms used by streaming platforms to automatically generate playlists to serve our purposes. The algorithms, as you're well aware, are becoming increasingly accurate. I know music aficionados would probably disagree with the use of algorithms, believing they'll ruin the pleasures of discovery and our unique tastes, but I think the machines are good enough to serve our purposes. With all this, the only caveat is we'll have to double-check with our religious law consultants to make sure we have the necessary permissions secured for using inappropriate music to achieve our virtuous goals. While we're on the subject of Americans, let me remind you, in case you've allowed yourselves to stay blind to these issues, of some of the various developments our American counterparts have made in this field. Did you know that their—or I guess for some of you I could say "your"—military uses private contractors to provide them with interrogation services? I mean, really, come on . . . I understand the economic model is different from ours—capitalism, privatization, outsourcing, and doing things as efficiently as possible—but really, private contractors in our field? How to trust them? And why let them reap the benefits? Unless there's some financial gain in these arrangements for whoever employs the contractors. I've seen that happening here in other government sectors, so I guess our models are not that different after all, despite appearances. Or maybe it's that by giving this job to private entities, the government can, if needed, absolve itself of any wrongdoing that might enrage the public. But again, as I said, I'm of the opinion that we should be proud, should hold our heads up high with regard to the work we do. The use of contractors is brought up in the book *Consequence*, the memoir of a former Abu Ghraib interrogator named Eric Fair. That's another funny thing about the Americans; they do whatever they like, then write books about how they did this or that and how sorry they are now and how they want to expose the system, as if the system would have existed without them and their cooperation in the first place. At least these kinds of writings are useful to us. This guy, Fair, talks about how their supervisors encouraged them to be creative, which is central to our practice too. However, he points out two practices we find no use for whatsoever in our system: one, filling out the right paperwork, and two, using softened language, such as "enhanced techniques," to refer to torture. You know, it is funny how shocked people still are when they learn about our practices, here in Iran and in the US. There are other differences, too, between our system and yours. Have you ever heard of General Karpinski? Well, let me tell you about her, in case you haven't. She was, according to your esteemed magazine the *New Yorker*, the only female commander in the war zone in Iraq, and she ran the Abu Ghraib prison. She was a business consultant before joining the prison team, and she is quoted saying that, for their prisoners, "living conditions now are better in prison than at home. At one point we were concerned that they wouldn't want to leave." Imagine that! We, at least, aren't foolish or audacious enough to say things like that. I believe another article mentioned that none of the interrogators in the prison considered their work "legally wrong," even though they might have considered it "morally wrong." Our system, luckily, has resolved this issue by fusing the moral and the legal, as every law we have is based on our theological teachings and values, aimed at the higher good of the people, so every act of our officers is not only legally but also morally valid and justifiable. I'm sorry, I keep getting carried away—but I imagine the similarities and differences between our system and those of our allies and enemies globally must be of interest to all of you too. Now, let's get back to the reason we're here: to celebrate our museum. I want to take a moment to acknowledge how thankful my team and I are to the project's financial sponsors. Without their contributions, none of this would have been possible. Even though there's still some work to be done, especially in the archive wing, we've come a very long way, and we're happy to be opening the museum, first with this tour, and we hope soon to the public. Over the course of the project, we've always made sure to have the best resources at our disposal, and to put everything to its most effective use. That's why I reached out far and wide, beyond our close circles, for support, not solely with regard to finances but also for consultations from scholars and experts in a wide range of fields, including museologists; archivists; librarians; audiovisual technicians and technology experts; psychologists specializing in torture, memory, and trauma studies; and veteran prison guards and former prisoners who were open to cooperating with us. A complete list of our sponsors is available at the back of the brochure you'll receive later, but here I want to express my gratitude to our largest donors Astan Quds Razavi, Mostazafan Foundation, the Cultural and Art Organization of Tehran Municipality, and the Islamic Revolutionary Guard Corps. I'm also particularly thankful to the spiritual and intellectual support of my colleagues at the Qasr Garden Museum and Ebrat Museum, which were prisons under the monarchy thoughtfully turned into museums a few years ago by our government to show our people some of the atrocities of the king and his men against those who spoke the truth and fought against them. Of course, as you might guess from my explanations so far, and as you yourself will shortly observe, the implementation and intentions of those torture museums are completely different than ours. Still, we benefited greatly from conversations and meetings with the directors and staff of both institutions, during which we addressed the shared issues we've all had to grapple with, so I want to express my gratitude to them. I believe it will be illuminating if I give you some examples of their work, to elaborate on how we're doing things differently. For example, our aim is to avoid the unthoughtful and sometimes even idiotic language used in the promotional materials of similar institutions. You might have already been to Ebrat Museum. If you haven't, I highly recommend it, though I should say, not to boast about our own accomplishments here, it is quite basic. Ebrat—the word means a "deterrent," a "lesson"— was a prison before our Revolution, as I said, so the building was originally constructed for that purpose, and it is amazing in that regard, a total Foucauldian panopticon, not merely an aesthetic choice but an architectural mechanism to implement terror and surveillance, allowing rulers to respond to the need for torture not just to punish criminals and stop crime from recurring in society but, more importantly, to demonstrate power. The building was designed, from what I've learned from the museum director, by German architects, who guaranteed that prisoners would be under nonstop surveillance and that no sound whatsoever would go beyond the walls of the building. Notice again the attention given here to sound. But let's return to the kind of language we use in delivering our message. I want to briefly analyze a promotional tourism video for Ebrat Museum, in which the presenter does an awful job poking fun at the torturers and interrogators of the previous regime. I am all for denouncing those imbeciles—they were horrifying figures—but with that kind of childish language? Do these presenters think they're comedians? Do they think they're playing it smart? It's ridiculous. If only they could learn to do things subtly, understand they don't need to be direct about everything with their audience, that they, too, can benefit from the arts of rhetoric and presentation. At one point, the presenter speaks of the officers' violence, using a tone and a word that will surely remind the audience of animals and beasts, and at another, he compares the experience of being imprisoned there to being on a haunted ride, you know, the ones in amusement parks— he calls it a "tunnel of horror." The worst is when he sits at a desk in the office there, explaining the connection between the intelligence service and foreign governments, including the forever-devilish forces of the US and Israel, and he turns toward some black-and-white pictures on the wall, pictures of the men who were once in charge, and says, sounding very official, "This committee included the most brutal and least sympathetic officers of the Mohammad Reza Pahlavi regime." OK, not too over the top, not yet, but listen to the rest. He then pauses and points to their faces with his pen and adds in a friendly tone, "And you can even tell how savage they are from their faces." Really?! And guess what! It doesn't stop there. He goes on to add that most of the men serving on the interrogation and torture committee, for the security of the monarchy, were, "based on the existing written and oral documentation . . . suffering from different types of mental disorders." See what

I'm saying? The people who wrote the script, or the pre-senter, or whoever the creative mind was behind the video, seemed unable to understand that by saying such things they were categorizing violence as something only certain types of officers and power holders were capable of, suggesting that those people were of a partic-ular type—sick, ugly, and disturbed—rather than see-ing them as normal and their work as the modus operandi. I know this is the inclination not just in this particular case but in general when it comes to seeing and decoding those who order and implement acts of horror, as evidenced by the very well-documented, well-discussed case of the Nazi officer Eichmann. Do you know that Hannah Arendt faced great backlash when she first noted that Eichmann was not an abnor-mal, evil human or nonhuman, arguing for her famous thesis on "the banality of evil"? My team and I are of the mind that supporting her thesis actually serves our pur-poses. If we introduce the ability to torture and interro-gate as an anomaly, then we're delegitimizing our work on several grounds. First, as I've been saying, it makes people see us as lunatics acting on our internal torments, not as members of a profession whose achievements are guided by serious research, innovation, and hard work. Second, it robs us of our humanity, which is something we want to resist with our PR materials, since it has hap-pened extensively throughout history and also in the social media discourse in the past several years, erasing the fact that we, too, have lives like everyone else in this world, that we experience love and fatigue and have dreams and all. And finally, this kind of language used in the video improperly stigmatizes those who are not beautiful or accepted according to socially defined, abstract standards. And add to all that the cheesiness of the ending! The last scene shows the presenter having fallen asleep on a bench in the museum, and we follow him into his dream of being a prisoner there, sitting in a cell, being violently dragged toward the interrogation room, and then being woken up by his cameraman, who tells him they're ready to leave. So awful . . . The video also brings in two former prisoners who now serve as tour guides at the museum. As living witnesses, they're key in establishing significant oral histories alongside the written documents. That is smart, I agree, but again, the presenter goes and makes the most obvious comment at the end about how he decided not to tell the story himself but rather to stand aside as a listener, to let the living proof speak for themselves, and then he tells the audience that now it's up to them to believe the men or not . . . A five-year-old would be smarter about playing with his audience. I'm not saying everyone in the business is like that presenter, but I've seen enough examples, especially on our state TV, that it irritates me. Anyway, speaking of sound, there's a sign in Ebrat Museum that reads "The only place where the walls will talk." I think this is a bad translation of the Persian. The future tense is not the right choice here. If there is a time for these walls to express themselves, that time is here and now, since the museum is already open. I mean, it has been many years since it was a prison, where acts of interrogation and torture were carried out, and as a museum, its function has been to showcase those past acts, so the verb should be present tense. And I feel that "speak" would be a better equivalent than "talk." "Will talk" does resonate more with an interrogator's voice, telling a prisoner "You will talk" or "I will make you talk," but that doesn't apply in the context of the sign or the walls. No one is forcing the walls to talk; they're simply filled with horror-struck voices of prisoners and other witnesses who couldn't express themselves during the prison years, voices that can now be released, are in fact supposed to be released, to tell and witness. Don't even get me started on the translation quality of many of the other documents in their archive, or the posters and the wall text. Some read as if they've been done by Google Translate. I don't understand why they can't hire capable translators, or at least have English speakers proofread and edit. We could discuss the damage such poor translations do for our international image, but for the sake of time, I want to move on to another important sound-related observation from the video. Both of the ex-prisoners, the tour guides, bring up sound several times at different moments. They remind viewers that the building was made so as not to allow any sound out, and they speak about how the sounds of the hallways' iron doors, and their locks being opened and closed many times, especially during the night, were mental torture for them, not allowing them to rest in their cells. One man actually wiggles a lock several times so we can hear the sound resonating throughout the space. The same man also imitates the voices of interrogators and officers, calling out and cursing the prisoners, pointing out that their voices, too, reverberated in the hallways. All I'm saying is that voice is quite central to how they remember and share these memories with the viewers. But God, the worst thing in that video was when one of the men spoke about the torture of female prisoners. He and the presenter are standing over the wax body of a female prisoner, covered in fake blood, lying on the floor and held by the wax figure of a male prison guard. The ex-prisoner–turned–tour guide speaks about how the interrogators used to pull the female prisoners' long hair—in the interrogation rooms, all along the hallways—and the women would howl and scream in pain, and the "sounds of their shrieks would reverberate in the cells," and, in his words, "hearing the women howl was one of the hardest kinds of torture for us." Then he adds, "I remember that I once personally broke down into tears . . . realizing that I was not able to do anything while a sister of ours, a woman, a fighter, who had ended up there under certain circumstances, was imprisoned, wondering why such things needed to hap-pen." I have heard this point from other former prison-ers as well, that hearing another prisoner being tortured or in pain was very disturbing, sometimes even harder than experiencing the pain themselves. But do you see what I'm saying about the gender dynamics here? Even in their sympathy, they speak about the female prisoner with this condescending undertone, as if woman is the weaker sex, as if she, unlike them, has ended up there by accident, as if she needs the male prisoners to be her saviors. It really pisses me off, and I know this isn't the place to express such grievances, especially among all of you, who are so ready to jump on our Islamic government for its oppression of women, but of course you won't be allowed to publish any of this without our preapproval. Also, I'm not going to let anyone or anything interfere with my museum opening and what I can do or say here; this is the height of my career and I don't care much what follows after this, as long as this achievement of mine gets the attention it deserves. Honestly, I'm at a point in life where I value nothing more than being true to myself, and, well, I couldn't agree more with your point of view when it comes to gender equality. I can give so many examples of gender bias, in both my personal and my professional lives. I hope to one day write a memoir focusing mainly on my grievances as a woman in this system, because injustices against women abound, especially in our line of work, and I want to share with others how I was able to smartly and innovatively navigate them and make space for myself and some of my female colleagues, and for many more women to come, I hope. You know what? I'm actually going to tell you a bit about that after I finish ripping apart this video . . . So the ex-prisoner then continues to narrate hearing the sound of the officers' laughter following the woman's shrieks, and the officers cursing and shouting at the prisoners inside the cells, telling them to listen carefully, that this was what the guards could do to the women; they could undress them and rape them if they wanted. His words, not mine. The ex-prisoner goes on to add, "It wasn't really unlikely that they would do this," but he emphasizes that they themselves didn't see anything. Wait for the next part—what follows is actually great material for some Freudian psychoanalysis. He's talking about the officers' words and their memories of the women's shrieks, and here he is interrupted by the presenter, who adds that to be subjected to and enduring these cries should have been "a psychological struggle" for the prisoners, but he says this with a slip of the tongue—instead of "psychological," he says, "freedom," because the two words in Persian sound alike, the former being "ravani" and the latter, "rahaii." I wonder if this means the presenter unconsciously sees the struggle for freedom as tied to one's psyche. Or is it that he sees the ex-prisoners' reaction to the women's pain as somehow related to their own freedom? I'm not really sure, but do you see what my all-female team and I have been working against? Anyway, both Ebrat Museum and Qasr Garden Museum were great case studies for us; we learned from their achievements and their failures and could then see more clearly what we wanted to do and what we definitely wanted to avoid. I'm also well aware that there are other museums around the world, such as the ones in Eastern Europe and in Chile, showcasing records and instruments of torture, highlighting the experiences of both the torturers and the prisoners, but our team decided to not visit these in person, to make sure we weren't too influenced by them and wouldn't be copying them, and instead would continue to do our own original thing here. The only one I, in a weak moment, couldn't resist, when I was in Berlin some time ago on a work trip, was the Topography of Terror. And oh my God, I honestly got goose bumps walking through the exhibition there. Some of the statements on the walls, you could just change minor identifying details and they could absolutely have been written about us; their vision and even the bureaucracy hit so close to home for me. What more proof do we need that what we're practicing here is all human, part and parcel of our nature. Anyway . . . Our plan is to send delegates to such institutions after opening the museum to the public and settling into things a bit with the operations of the different wings, including the main exhibition halls and the archives, to build up some international collaborations—for example, to do exchange programs for the exhibitions and our archival materials, invite guest speakers, and the like. Domestically, as my team and I found some momentum, we began to get attention from different organizations and higher-ups. One of the most enticing proposals for collaboration came from the Islamic Revolution Document Center, or, as we call it, the IRDC. They suggested that we join forces and establish their torture documents subdivision in return for receiving their institutional support and access to their resources. The other institution that came forward was the State Prisons and Security and Corrective Measures Organization. To be frank, their proposal was kind of aggressive; it didn't even sound much like a proposal. They stated that since some of our research was carried out in prisons and was thus under the umbrella of their organization, we needed to officially be part of their system, work in accordance with their rules and regulations, and hand the management of our establishment over to them after inauguration. Can you believe the audacity? Give my baby to them to do whatever they want to do with it? Over my dead body. First, some of the torture techniques we've been investigating are experimented with outside our official prisons, in secret detention centers housed in unidentified buildings; you might have heard the term "safe houses"—yes, that's what I'm talking about. So the State Prisons and Security and Corrective Measures Organization doesn't really have the right to make such a pronouncement. When I announced that we wanted to remain independent, the directors there were furious and threatened to ban my team from accessing prisons to collect data on the ground, and even to stop our operations. Luckily for us, though, I had the foresight to secure the support of a few high-level, extremely influential people in key positions at the very beginning of my project, including religious, financial, and political figures, who, I'm sure you understand, want to remain publicly anonymous, whom no one dares to agitate. Otherwise, as a woman working with a mainly female team, we would have had no chance of survival in this climate, and besides—I probably shouldn't tell you this, but to hell with it—I had seen enough examples of successful projects, from factories to businesses to educational and arts organizations, especially when women were involved, that were confiscated by the so-called gentlemen in charge to ensure that the prestige and any financial gain belonged to no one but them. Thank God we were able to . . . What's the phrase you use in English? . . . Yes, nip their bullying in the bud. Presently, we are part of the larger family of the National Museum of the Islamic Revolution and Holy Defense, which represents a history of the Iran-Iraq war alongside other key battles of the Islamic Republic against both domestic and international enemies, a mission that aligns very well with our own. I also appreciate functioning under their umbrella since they, too, underline not only a transferring of knowledge but also, per my conversations with the directors, the creation of multimedia experiential tours for their visitors. Since our work is quite specialized and extensive, however, I negotiated, with the help of several insightful lawyers, a contract that, with regard to our unique vision and future plans, allows us to sustain our independence while still benefitting from their material and immaterial resources. Now, let's get back to the importance of our work in modernizing the pedagogy of torture.

Darius Rejali explains to us that torture is taught through "informal ways," what he calls "backroom apprenticeships." This method has historically had benefits as well as some drawbacks, including what I noted earlier regarding a lack of systematic evaluation methodology. That's a concern for sure, but to be honest, it's not our main one. Especially in this day and age, the age of the internet and global connections, when these informal ways of teaching and learning through back channels, or the so-called open-source materials, are utilized more and more frequently, we can see that they are quite efficient in allowing wide access while diversifying and innovating educational contents. And when it comes to evaluations, they, too, can happen in newer, more fluid and in-depth ways. We can, for example, have our documentations of the torture sessions analyzed by experts. We can do qualitative interviews with the torturers themselves and get firsthand narrative feedback, force prisoners to do qualitative exit surveys before being freed, or evaluate our methods through analyzing the museum audience's reactions to the exhibited sounds from our sessions. Such methods, I believe, give us more holistic feedback than older methods that might be more efficient and easier to implement on a wide scale. As for teaching and learning, my key ambition for the museum is not to teach the methodology of torturing, though that is happening too, through the archives, but more so to find the most effective ways to instill in our new apprentices the right mindset and emotional state so they can build up the necessary stamina and not lose their nerve doing this kind of work, especially over time. Training their emotional intelligence, you may say. Having them spend time at the museum is a good testing mechanism. If the trainees can withstand being here for several long sessions without breaking down, building up their perseverance, or even better, if they get excited in our space and begin to imagine what they'll be capable of and share what they can contribute to the industry, then we can seriously consider them as eligible candidates, worth the time and effort to train expansively, worth passing our secrets on to, whether orally and informally, or as we say idiomatically in Persian, "chest to chest," or through more official pedagogical methods. In a sense, the museum can act as a vetting space and help us not only with choosing the best candidates but also with increasing security and decreasing the chance of having defectors among us, since even one weak or infectious link can cause irreversible damage. All in all, our intention here is to set a precedent in the field with regard to documentation, pedagogy, evaluation, and presentation. We want to move away from secrecy, since, as Rejali notes, when it comes to torture, there is a lack of expansive documentation and systematic evaluation, which means that either no data exists, or, when it does, it is kept secret, so there's an urgency for us to fill the gap and share the incredible knowledge we've amassed. As I said earlier, my stance is that we have to hold our heads up high and be proud of what we do. Who can really touch us? No one. Everyone is benefitting from torture; this is how it has been forever; this is what we, as humans, are inclined to do. We just do it in different ways and call it different names. So we shouldn't let others write our narrative for us, even though what has historically been happening is that any kind of research in this field has been based on either public information or rumors. What that means is, the narrative is completely biased and shaped by scholars' abstract philosophies, which are not necessarily backed up by empirical findings or, at best, are based on what researchers are finding out secondhand or from former prisoners, which might not yield the most up-to-date data. What is curious and even baffling to me is that, according to Rejali, "governments read scholars instead of analyzing their own data" on torture. It's kind of funny, and really a missed opportunity, though I see how this arises from the complexity of the situation. In the case of our project, for example, even though my team is comprised of highly vetted scholars and researchers in different disciplines, we still cannot allow them direct access to collect data by sitting in our sessions, nor can we create the desired scientific research conditions, such as having control and treatment groups inside our prisons or secret interrogation centers. This reminds me of—you might have already heard of it too—the famous Stanford Prison Experiment, which was carried out in the early 1970s and involved selected subjects playing the role of prisoners and prison guards. Does anyone know about this? Yes, right; I thought you'd be familiar. The experiment revealed that everyone is prone to inflicting violence on others, the same violence for which the public has demonized the people in my field. Everyone would do what we do, if put in the right context, if given permission and responsibility. The experiment revealed the human beings' natural desire to do what we do as professionals, though, as professionals, we do gain the skill sets to do our jobs in the best possible way. In the words of Rejali—let me put up the slides and read to you this section; it's pretty good: "Professional torturers colonize bureaucratic, judicial, and legislative bodies designated to supervise them, making oversight difficult" and "civil servants cannot exercise selective control once they have licensed armed men to exercise unlimited power over individuals." As a result, "the populations liable to be tortured, however narrowly defined at first, grow over time." Knowing all this, along with our emphasis on creativity and prompt decision-making, we are actually hesitant to micromanage our torturers and interrogators. With regard to the protocols of our project, the researchers tell us what kind of data they need, and we collect it and provide it to them. Then, based on these materials, they come up with the most effective plans for how to assess as well as present the outcomes of our procedures. Maybe this is just as good a time as any for me to get back to telling you about the gender dynamics in my profession, how I overcame some of the hurdles in this overly patriarchal system, just *some of* them, and found my way through the maze. And I'll also tell you a bit more about our attempts at gender equity in this project. I'm aware that this is not directly related to the museum, but believe me, it sure is in indirect ways, and since I have your ear, I'm going to take full advantage of it and also tell you a bit about myself. You are well aware by now that although I have deep respect for what we do here, I have real problems with how my fellow female colleagues and I have been treated over the years. One thing that amuses me is that in a system that believes deeply in the separation of sexes, female prisoners are still primarily being interrogated and tortured by male officers. The female officers are given roles that are either on the sidelines or, if of any importance, merely for the sake of show—so for example, they give you a mouth-filling title or even make you director of this or that unit, but still every decision you make needs to go through the male higher-ups. No real meaningful changes have been made, for that matter, in the hiring system, and nothing has been done to the glass ceiling that hinders the young, smart cadets coming in from moving up the ladder, despite their excellent performances. If a unit is sent to arrest women who are accused of political activities or suspected to have harmed our national security, female officers are sent in along with the men so they can touch the women or put handcuffs on them, to make sure we remain within our religious guidelines for mixed-gender relationships. We still don't have enough female officers, however, and more often than not it's our male colleagues who find themselves on the scene and have to deal with these situations, so the religious concerns can be overlooked, it seems, whenever needed. Emergency situations demand emergency measures and lenience on such matters. In the women's wards, the lower-rank guards who interact with the prisoners on a day-to-day basis are of course female, but more complex tasks, including interrogation and torture, are still carried out by men. There is now a female police unit, and women can study to become officers. I'm sure you have all seen images of the Iranian female police force, in black veils, in formation or in action; I would say the most famous pictures out there are the ones by Abbas Kowsari, taken some years ago during their graduation from the police academy, holding guns, marching, chasing, or, in the one everyone talks about, hanging from ropes and scaling a wall. I've seen that image used over and over by Western media throughout the years, in so many different contexts. You guys love those images. They fit so well with your stereotype of us as dark, violent, backward threats; you've even made our black veil such a threatening symbol. You love those images much more than the images of so many other women in this country, the ones who have actually proven to be a problem for us, and yes, you do show them from time to time, to substantiate your narrative of Iranian women rebelling and all, fighting for their rights, but even with those stories, the use of images depicting us adhering to the full Islamic dress code, in

threatening poses, is still prevalent. It would be interesting if someone actually did some research on the imag-
ery of women from Iran, or even from the larger Middle
East, used by the Western media, to see what kind of
conscious and unconscious narratives they promote.
Scholar Sharif Gemie, in his book *Women's Writing and
Muslim Societies,* studies the book covers of memoirs by
women from the Middle East in diaspora and talks
about how the covers mostly show the women either
from behind or looking down, adding that even when
the eyes are shown, they seem passive, saddened, or
powerless, never with the kind of sparks that imply a
sense of agency. If I'm not mistaken, he even notes that
there are several instances of the same set of eyes being
used on the covers of different books. Imagine that. I
mean, we women in the Middle East are suffering on
both fronts, from the patriarchal men here and the
Western gaze, which orientalizes and diminishes us.
Even the cover of *Time,* when they picked Iranian
women as their heroes of the year, showed them from
behind. And mind you, as is always the case, the likes of
me and my wonderful team have no place in such categories and praises of women: it's all about the women
we're fighting against here, not us. Anyway, let's get
back to the story of our neglected female forces . . .
There's another role assigned to us, that of undercover
agents, that has always made me furious. I mean, there's
nothing especially wrong with going undercover and
playing different roles, but when I explain, you'll under-

stand, because our female officers are not going undercover the same way as men. They're mainly assigned to
use their bodies and their seductive powers to trap or spy
on the men in positions of power. You see what the problem is, right? Our women have to marry these guys,
either through a regular marriage or as temporary wives
through sigheh, or sometimes, though rarely, become
their lovers, like in your countries, to direct them toward
or away from a planned course of action, and that is
totally OK as part of the job and demands such mental
fortitude and strategic navigation, but the problem I
have with all this is that the men in our force almost
never get assigned to carry out similar missions. It kind
of makes sense, I know, because there are more men
whom we need to surveil and manipulate, but even that
on its own is a symptom of the larger patriarchal system.
So you see, it's quite a vicious circle. This brings up
another issue for me, reveals a paradox, if I may. In many
discourses around women serving in positions of power,
such as in the presidency or in judiciary roles, one of the
arguments raised against them, besides the religious
considerations, is that women are emotional and thus
unreliable, that they cannot be trusted to make sound
judgements and fair decisions, but nobody in these circles ever mentions that the men in positions of power
make wrong decisions all the time, fuck things up for
various reasons, among them their own desires and
impulses, especially the perverse sexual ones, and these
men and their patriarchal system find different ways to

push everything under the carpet—is that a phrase you use as well? I'm not sure; we use it in Persian when we want to talk about trying to hide something, putting it out of sight, which these men do no matter what to make sure their vulnerable individual and collective egos are not hurt. I'm sure the women here in the group agree with me, right? I can see your smiles. The situation might be a bit better in your countries, because women there have been able to push for some changes, but even so, I would say that gender equity remains quite disappointing; the mistrust toward putting women in positions of power is huge, beyond imagination. Anyway, as I was saying, the women in our industry have been widely deployed to keep an eye on the men in power, which reveals that the male decision-makers themselves know that their male counterparts are going to fall for the female agents. Well, many of them—I shouldn't generalize. I've met a handful of men in my life who have proven to be exceptions. I won't go as far as to call them gentlemen, as is the tradition in such contexts, but I would say that some men have succeeded in rising above and beyond the prejudices of their gender and the power machine behind it, and perhaps that's why none of these men lasted in our line of work or similar government positions for that long; they disappeared or migrated or deteriorated mentally and physically. The term used for these female undercover forces is "parastoo," meaning "swallow," as in the bird, which those of you who understand Persian—if I remember correctly, a few of you do—already know. It's mind-blowing to me, the fact that you cover the news of a country, call yourselves experts, without having access to its language. Imagine if it were reversed and we did that to your countries and the news coming out of them! Anyway . . . Despite all the limitations put on the women in our forces, I came to meet many capable ones during my years of service. In the interrogation rooms, however, there were no female officers in charge, even if we were allowed to be present to carry out lower-level tasks, until I came along. And to be honest, I, too, had to shadow the men for years and years before they trusted me to do the work on my own. To achieve that, I quickly learned that the best strategy was to play the role of the mother figure, because mothers are considered sacred in our culture—we say "Paradise is under mothers' feet"— and because most men in my country—I don't know about yours, but I'd imagine it's much the same—have complicated bonds with their mothers, even if they don't know it or know it but don't acknowledge it. So it was by perfecting that role over the years that I succeeded in pushing my way further and further into the system. You might ask yourself, if you're good reporters and researched your topic, how come the men allowed me that? Didn't they propose to me? Didn't they want me to become their wife or their lover? To be honest, I do have a strong ally in the system, one of our top interrogators and torturers. We've been legally married for many years, and though it has not been a conventional one done out of love or belief in the institution of marriage, we have not let anyone sense that. In the eyes of everyone, we have been a power couple, so no one dared say or do anything inappropriate, put forth any indecent proposals or criticisms whatsoever. To let you in on a secret, he and I simply arrived at that marriage arrangement for professional reasons. He saw my potential as well as the challenges in front of me. When he first came to me to talk about the marriage thing, I was so angry and defensive, even hated him for a while, but little by little I realized that the two of us joining forces would be a match made in heaven. We married, developed the illusion of intimacy, and were able to fool everyone. To be honest, over the years we had so much fun with our game of pretense—it brought us so close and created a unique relationship. But enough about my private life. You don't need to know more than that. The goal was for the two of us to join forces to expand our access to what was going on around us, in both the male and female arenas. As you can see, our plan definitely worked in my favor. Our union proved indispensable to me as I worked to gradually shift the gender imbalance in the industry. The disparity wasn't reflected in just the makeup and roles of the prison staff and officers but also in the methods used against female and male prisoners. In interrogations of female prisoners, the male officers, more often than not, used sexual slurs, and even though they never did this while I was present, I've heard it recounted enough times to know that it is true. I've heard they even went, in some cases, as far as forcing the women to make the sounds they would make during sexual acts, pretending they were having an orgasm. There have also been rumors, especially more recently, of physical rape, of our female and male prisoners alike, but that is, I assure you, nonsense, totally untrue: rape is, for us, a red line never to be crossed. But I have been pissed off that the kind of actions I was just describing were always applied manyfold to women. It just rubs me the wrong way, this disgusting dual positioning toward women: on the one hand, there's the oversexualization of women who are strangers to my male colleagues or other men in power, and on the other, the portrayal of women as saints, not even part of the material world, when it comes to these same men's own mothers, sisters, wives, and daughters. There is never an in-between. We, the women, can either be whores or saints or not women at all. Honestly, I have no idea what they think or fantasize about those of us who have professional lives of any kind. Where do they see us? What kind of women are we to them? They never know what to do with us, never let us just be. I've worked in the system for more than three decades, from my mid-twenties on, and I'm frustrated by how little and slow the changes in treatment of women have been. Besides the union with my partner in crime, what truly helped me, especially in the early months of my career, was the mentorship I got from one woman in the system. I was just an entry-level guard at the women's prison, and one day, an older woman, a janitor there, took me aside and gave me the most important advice—advice that has sustained me for all the years of my work. She had entered the workforce in the early, chaotic days after the Revolution and had remained in the prison system ever since, amazingly, without anyone ever questioning her presence there. I was young and had no experience, neither professionally nor with men, and even though I was very stubborn and hotheaded back then, something in her manner and her tone made me pause and listen carefully, and I still remember what she told me. I guess her secret was the grandmotherly aura she had when she did her rounds, chatting with prisoners and staff, offering them all some kind of support, oftentimes with simply a word or a look, observing everything that was going on while also always keeping herself quiet as a mouse, almost invisible. God bless her soul, she passed away just a few months ago. She had such humility; she never wanted me to give her credit anywhere for her role as my unofficial mentor. Oh how I wish she were here today to hear me and witness the fruit of my resilience at this inauguration. Actually, when I started this project, I asked her to join us, to move from the prison to the offices where we had settled. The job would have been easier than what she was doing there, and she could have just been in charge of the kitchenette and minor cleaning, but she refused, saying she wanted to spend the last few years of her life where she felt most at home, close to the prisoners. I don't know how she knew she would soon leave us, but she did. As I was saying, one day she took me aside while I was walking through the hallway in the women's ward, going from one office to another, files under my arms, very much frustrated by something my male superior had just said. I didn't tell her a thing, but being who she was, she somehow knew the moment I murmured a hello to her, and a "Khasteh nabashid," a phrase you don't have in English but that is so prevalent in spoken Persian, in so many different contexts, and literally translates to "May you not be tired." During my years abroad, I always found myself missing that phrase so much. It always comes in handy, especially if you want to build rapport with, for example, the store clerk or the handyman or the admin people in offices. The old woman didn't say a word, merely grabbed the files from me and walked away, and I followed her without opposing or making a scene, and she went into the female staff bathroom and closed the door after I entered. She looked me in the eye and, with an authority I never saw in her before that day or after, told me, "You are like my daughter. And if you want to survive in this place and profession, you need to listen to what I am telling you . . . The Qajar women of the court were the ones truly ruling this country, from behind the scenes, quietly, pretending to be shadow players. Learn from them. Also, remember that our system respects women only as mothers, so you need to empty yourself of your sexuality, become the mother to them all, the officers, the interrogators, the judges, even to your female colleagues, and that's how

you can push forth through them, make them trust you."
So I took to heart the advice she gave me. And then,
much later, my marriage helped me—what's the phrase
you use?—yes, to go the extra mile in my career. Despite
our struggles for gender equity taking forever to really
affect the foundation of our system, you can see there
have been some meaningful results in the past few years:
the success of female interrogators doubling as TV
anchors in our state media who have helped our
public-facing coverage of confessions and productions
exposing plots against the state; the female officers who
have been indispensable to our "morality police" units;
and most recently, our female antiriot forces, fully
trained both physically and psychologically, who officially started their mission during the latest round of
protests in our country. As this new iteration of public
unrest was led by large numbers of women and young
girls who are our enemies, we needed the full-force presence of our female officers more than ever, so it was a
great opportunity for us to break new ground and prove
ourselves even further. For those of you who are around
for the next few days and going on the guided tours
we've arranged for you in our beloved city, I suggest you
keep an eye out for them. You know, I'll actually ask
your tour leaders to make sure you can meet with them
or, if possible, see them in action. That would be good
publicity for us. These female special forces have
exceeded my expectations, and I'm so proud of them. In
one particular case, a so-called activist, Leyla Mirghafari,

who was arrested in the streets, described in an Instagram post how one of our female colonels put her hands around her neck, exerting force, telling her she would kill her. Seeing the fear in the eyes of this woman, even when she recounted this after being released on bail, made me proud of how far we've come. For these special forces, we've even been able to design a more versatile dress code, approved by our religious consultants, which gives our female officers the freedom to do their jobs to their full potential, though the ones in the black veils have also been great at carrying out their missions on the ground. As one of the pioneering high-ranking female officers in this field, I have always aspired to change the working conditions for future generations of female interrogators and torturers, especially considering that we have more need for them, as we're increasingly bringing in more and more female prisoners from a wide range of groups: women's rights activists, social workers, union leaders, laborers, saleswomen, journalists, lawyers, artists, students, even ordinary housewives; you name it. And I don't know if you're aware of this, but the age group is also consistently younger and younger . . . I guess our women and our youth have been more susceptible to the discourse of the West and what they have been fed about freedom and empowerment, duplicating Western white feminism, instead of being intelligent and creating a feminism to align with our own traditions and background, serving us, at this moment, in this geographical location. Among our prisoners, we also have the occasional dual citizens, some of whom arrive in town for suspicious research projects, especially in the humanities, or as journalists or artists. I remember a few of them in particular: one was investigating—imagine the audacity—the most intimate aspect of our women's lives, their sexual behavior. Her book title was *Passionate Uprisings*, I think, and the subtitle, something about sexual revolution. I don't recall who it was by, unfortunately, but you can search for it easily enough. And there was an author who wrote a memoir called *Lipstick Jihad* . . . Both of these women and many more were pretty savvy about getting around our surveillance network and somehow managed to work under the radar and gather all their data, despite our attempts to limit and threaten them. This was, of course, many years ago now, at a time when we had less leeway in the extent of our legal crackdowns against these infiltrators, when we had to act more discreetly so as not to arouse the suspicion of even our own higher-ups. I assure you, however, our responses to these scholars and journalists affiliated with foreign institutions have in the recent years become diligent and effective, so many do not dare to come back here to continue their work. You can tell even from the titles of these two books, which are just two examples of the kinds of narratives these writers, oftentimes women, want to push for, that they are obsessed with making everything that relates to us and our lives about war and jihad and uprising, on the one hand, and about the body and sex, on the other. You saw examples of these kinds of language and narratives in the coverage of the most recent rebellions against us in much of your own media as well. I would argue that this is a new branch of neo-Orientalism, a repackaging of the age-old tags you've used for us, seeing us as either sexual and exotic or savages and barbarians, a people with all kinds of behavioral complexes constantly fighting with one another, as if Westerners were such civilized saints, living in eternal peace. I'm sorry to be blunt about this, but there is no way around the hypocrisy here, though you, our esteemed guests, have been good about exposing such issues, and that's why you're here now, to be the first to tour our museum. Most of your governments and even your people see us as no more than an underdeveloped third-world country. Even when the social activism and women's rights movements you yourselves advocate for happen here in my country or in other countries in the Middle East, you have a hard time acknowledging them. We clearly witnessed your hesitations and silence in the face of the recent demonstrations here, which we, with God's hand behind us, were able to suppress. Even in your so-called sympathy and support for the recent rioters disrupting public order and threatening our national stability, you don't see them as your equals. Otherwise—I'm sorry to break this to you—you should have already tied your own fights, particularly those led by the feminists and the liberals, to theirs; by now, you could have turned them all into one unified global phenomenon, the people against those of us running the well-established systems of power. But thank God, this has not happened, and I don't see it happening anytime soon either. And please don't try to argue otherwise and tell me such discrimination doesn't exist. Even some of your own colleagues, the journalists covering the most recent Ukraine war, let it slip at the beginning of the attacks, saying the war was abhorrent and needed to be immediately stopped, when so many wars have been ongoing in our region for so long, because, as they said in the news, Ukrainians are Europeans, blond and modern and civilized, unlike the people in this region, or as we say in idiomatic Persian, because their blood is more colorful than ours. Anyhow, enough with all that. As I was saying, with my vision for gender equity in the field, I had a twofold plan for our museum project. First I reached out mainly to women to join my team for imagining and constructing the museum. I was a bit worried in the beginning that it would be a challenge to find enough expert women in these fields, and if there were enough, they might not want to lend their expertise to such a project. You can guess, of course, that the initial concern was totally baseless, despite the forever rehashed popular discourse that there are not enough female experts working in various fields. As to my other concern, let me tell you, there are women you can buy off the same way you can most men; offer them enough power and money, and they're just as willing as the men to dive into whatever shit you're putting out in front of them. This is something I've learned: being willing to fight for feminist values, such as equality and collaboration instead of hierarchy and domination, and removing the glass ceiling, isn't necessarily tied to being a woman or a man; some women can act more aligned with patriarchal values than men themselves, perhaps because of a desire to make up for being women and to prove themselves to their male counterparts, buying into their foul, competitive mindset. But I didn't want that kind of environment or those kinds of people for my team. I wanted women who were invested in imagining other kinds of communities, ones that would empower all of us, not one individual or group at the expense of others and not out of a desire for money or hierarchical powers. That didn't mean I wasn't going to compensate them well, not at all; that was one of my central concerns, to provide these women with the financial security they deserve. I just wanted to secure shared foundations and push my desired framework and design forward, so I needed to work with women who had the right vision and values to bring to our museum, but finding them was kind of tricky, because for ages, men have held the thrones in this field. But I'm happy to announce we've had some breakthroughs. For example, we've implemented feminist and feminine approaches in our architectural design, in our narrative strategies, and in our archival presentation of documents and objects, as well as in addressing our audience's needs and encouraging them to join in a world-building process, which I'll explain further when we step into the main section of the museum. You know what, let me just give you a hint, since it's pretty exciting, and I'm so proud of my team for aspiring to it. With regard to world-building, we decided to create one wing in the museum *not* dedicated to the past, to a historicized view, but rather to looking toward the future—for example, by opening new avenues for experimentation and developing new techniques in collaboration with our visitors, inviting them to either write down ideas or record their voices if they have suggestions for us to try, since crowdsourcing oftentimes brings in ideas that no one individual or team could come up with alone. The younger generation in particular is so good at this type of engagement. I believe this has something to do with their existence in the virtual world and their imagining so many possibilities in that realm. But we'll talk more about that later. The second way I've tried to improve gender equity and move away from the mainstream patriarchal system is in how I've tried to distribute authority within my team. We've done our best to work as a collective, avoiding hierarchies and allowing everyone equal opportunity to put their fullest potential on the table, with me mainly playing the role of the facilitator. This structure has had its own challenges, but it has also been an enriching learning experience, especially since many of our team members are younger women and are pretty amazing, bringing forth novel perspectives not only on how the museum should be materialized but also on how we should run things around here. Of course, as the facilitator, I still had to be at the helm and oversee operations, but this is different from how things are run in the traditional masculine power structures within which most of us have had to work all throughout our lives. I strongly oppose the need for a boss and for constant micromanagement, because it stifles the team members' creativity and efficiency. I went with this alternative model because I knew it would allow me to learn so much from these younger talents, and learn I did. I'm not like my male colleagues, who pretend to be the best in the field, knowing everything and thus having no need to learn from anyone; it is hell working with and especially under them. As a result, from the very beginning of the project, I wanted to avoid recreating such toxic dynamics in my team and aimed for more open, horizontal approaches, letting everyone know that their vision and creativity were welcome. When you step into the main section of the museum, you'll see that we've dedicated a room to introducing each of our team members and their role in the project, except for those who preferred to remain anonymous for reasons of either security or humbleness. You'll also find a complete list of their names, except those few, at the end of the pamphlet you've been handed. I wanted to ensure I'm showing my gratitude to each and every one of these women who have been indispensable to my learning process and growth. As I've mentioned, examining the theory behind what I've been doing hands-on for so many years has been key to making this museum come to life in this unique shape and form. Learning about the history, philosophy, global trends, the newest methodologies, and the psychology behind torture and interrogation, along with the critical, oftentimes controversial conversations among academics, has been life changing. I had no idea there were such extensive studies on the topic. Of course, much of the knowledge we acquired will not be directly on display in the museum, but it has definitely informed our behind-the-scenes operations, maximizing and diversifying the impact on our audience and ensuring the museum's success. As I noted, one of our germinal texts was Darius Rejali's *Torture and Democracy;* I highly recommend it. Pretty early on in the project, I put together a mandatory reading group facilitated by one of our best political scientists, so the whole team could gain a shared knowledge and language base, to borrow from our software engineering colleagues, for both our back-end and front-end activities. There were also two other important Iranian authors whose work in Persian inadvertently provided us with more in-depth historical accounts from the previous generation of torturers and tortured prisoners, going back to the 1980s: Iraj Mesdaghi, who has written several books on the topic, and Monireh Baradaran, whose memoirs we found very useful. I want to hereby offer my gratitude, even though that might sound counterintuitive and would perhaps be offensive to them, but honestly, their books have been so helpful. There were many other books as well, of course, and we provide a full bibliography in our educational wing and have copies of many of them in the center's library, which is a lovely space for doing work and additional research, for those who are interested, both on a global scale and in the context of Iran, though for the books in Persian, you may need to use the services of reliable translators. I want to emphasize "reliable" here, because if you're not careful and use one of the Iranians in diaspora who've become servants of either the political agenda of the West and their lobbyists or, honestly, servants of their own selfish desire for money and success, they might add or subtract from the documents as they wish, so make sure your translator is someone you can trust. We actually offer services from in-house certified and trusted translators, and you can talk to our librarians if you find yourself needing one. To solve this problem long term, we have plans for commissioning translations, during the next phase of our work, and publishing these books in English so we can have them on hand in the library. One thing I wanted to clarify, now that we're on the topic of sources, is that you might have noticed during this welcome speech that I've been mainly referring to Western ones. That's not because we haven't relied on Iranian and local sources, but rather because I've wanted to be attentive to you, my audience, and your contexts, thus presenting to you mainly sources and situations that you either are already familiar with or can verify more easily. If you're curious to know more about our Persian sources, please let our lovely librarians know.

Next I want to remind all of you of the necessity of building a museum of torture that is facing toward both the past and the future. Our research shows that interrogators, and not just ours but all of them, all around the world, learn from one another, but interestingly, they do not 100 percent imitate one another or previous methods. Rejali discusses how even when torturers rely on methods taken from their own past traumatic experiences and memories, doing to others the worst things done to them, they never do the exact same thing, but something similar, always making sure to innovate. The reason, according to Rejali, is first to differentiate themselves and prove their individuality, and second to present themselves as people who are not as evil as their predecessors. Part of this, I guess, is due to a complicated web of feelings of guilt and shame, as well as the exhilaration that comes from the insatiable thirst for agency and power. It reminds me of something I once heard at a reading on one of my travels abroad. The book was by a scholar of Jewish literature, whose name escapes me now, who investigated alternative possibilities for the establishment of the Zionist state, or, as he called it, the Jewish state, locations and scenarios that were once considered but were never realized, because, as we all know, they ended up brutally occupying Palestine, basically stealing people's lands and homes, taking their lives, to this day. Even though the talk wasn't directly on torture methods, I couldn't avoid making certain associations; on the one hand, because of our investment in the plight of our Palestinian brothers and sisters, and on the other, because the Zionist regime occupying the holy Quds is one of the leading forces in torture in our day and age, literally running the world's biggest open-air prison, or, if I want to be more accurate, concentration camp, a term used by one of their own scholars, sociologist Baruch Kimmerling. Anyway, after emphasizing that he himself strongly condemned the human rights abuses against Palestinians, the scholar explained that many Israelis today do not really see themselves as forces of evil, because for them, evil and torture are what the Nazis did to them—well, to their ancestors, really—during the Holocaust, meaning the gas chambers and the camps, and anything short of that doesn't count, doesn't dent their consciences enough to disrupt their sleep or make them rise to fight for human rights. How can anyone see the conditions under which our fellow Palestinians live and not recognize that as torture? The limitations on their right to movement; their lack of access to clean water, electricity, and medical care; the continuous overtaking of their land; the constant violence against them; the attacks to their subjectivity and humanity—I could go on and on. Let me clarify something here, though, because I'm sure this may raise questions for some of you. You may have heard some of our officials publicly questioning the Holocaust, but that's mainly a strategy to help us with our agendas, and most of us, I should assure you, not only do not question the Holocaust but also are very much aware of it and its impact on reshaping our world today. But that's a conversation for another time. As to encouraging our torturers to hold on to their sense of agency, we find feeding their imaginations and assisting them in growing more and more original is hugely beneficial to our industry. So we don't want to teach too prescriptively or regulate things too tightly, because the creativity of our mid- and lower-level agents is an integral element of achieving the mastery we're aiming for. Plus, this approach allows us to reign over and traumatize the young torturers as well as the tortured. When they're put in charge of making decisions on a case-by-case basis, they get a sense of individuation, autonomy, and achievement, which is exhilarating to them, without them realizing that they're simultaneously being pulled into the trap we've set for them. Anything to achieve our mission. Little by little, they get stuck in the dirty work, addicted to the adrenaline rush brought on by their violent power, but that power is merely an illusion, or partial, because they are, in the end, puppets in our hands, even though we want them to think otherwise. All of them. The tortured and the torturer. This emphasis on creativity and individual innovation is, today, more urgent than ever before, because with increased access to information about different interrogation and torture techniques, whenever we bring prisoners in, they already have some level of knowledge about what to expect and, consequently, some level of conscious or unconscious training on possible defense mechanisms on how to survive our moves, to some extent. So I'm all for imagination. We face two very opposite impulses here, however: our goal is to keep our own and our torturers' imaginations alert and alive, continuously flourishing, while doing all in our power to take away or limit our captives' imaginations, to keep them from going too far in grooming their wishes and desires, whether for their survival and sanity, for their joy and pleasure, or toward their freedom, literal or symbolic. We need to focus their attention and energy on negative, terrifying events and overwhelm them, so they have no opportunity for generative thought or dreaming about building a brighter future. In this way, we keep their bodies and minds and hearts all confined. And brilliantly, the same thing works on the larger population, outside the prison system. If we keep bombarding the public with horrifying news, or even better, create vague circumstances of terror, they constantly need to look over their shoulders, calculate their every step only from guesses, and in the end they'll be left with no energy to build different, better futures for themselves individually or collectively. One of my team members recently brought to my attention a video of an interview with journalist, author, and Nobel Prize winner Svetlana Alexievich, in which she discusses the training of Belarusian security forces. I found some of her language problematic, but I want to quote her here to show just how much we share with many of our colleagues around the world. She says in the interview, of course this is based on the translated subtitles, "At first I even thought that the people who were so cruel to Belarusians weren't Belarusians." I disagree with the use of the word "cruel," since we do what we do for the security of our land and our national interests. But what's interesting is that we've heard similar comments on the streets in Iran—our undercover agents report people saying that we're importing our security forces from other countries, or that our forces are drugged. They don't believe we, their fellow countrymen and women, could in our natural state be as forceful as we are, which is sad, because we're simply not being given enough credit. One look at the state of the so-called opposition in diaspora, and the tendencies they reveal from time to time, whether on the ground during protests against us or online, their petite enmities, their shortsightedness—their violence, verbal and sometimes even physical, against each other—their desire for power and mastery long before they've won a battle against us, should be enough for people to understand that this is all just part of our nature, this is who we are—basically, human beings. As to employing forces from our neighbors in the region, even if such statements were true, what's the problem with allies having each other's backs in times of need? Or using medication to help motivate and strengthen us, the way vitamins and antidepressants do? Alexievich continues, let me put up the slide and quote her verbatim: "I had photos of what they had done. Of the wounds and all . . . they caused real disabilities there. And even to come up with those cruelties, you could only compare them to

Stalin or to the Gestapo. That's how inconceivable they were. . . . And, of course, we asked ourselves in what cages those dogs had been raised. Now we know that Lukashenko not only prepared the weapons, not only prepared the state-of-the-art tech, to scare people into submission, he also did a lot to groom those people—the people he hired into SWAT, the Suvorov Military School, and the police. There were special lessons there, we now call them 'dehumanization lessons.' . . . They had implemented a whole science of dehumanization there." I prefer to think about it not as "dehumanizing," but rather as pulling out the hidden layers of humanity. Obviously, our training programs make us powerful not just in our work inside the prisons but also on the streets, especially as the number of street protests and daily acts of disobedience keep rising. Training our torturers' imaginations and grooming their abilities to tell stories is key from another perspective as well, because, according to our go-to scholar Darius Rejali, interrogators tend to describe their "fantasies as facts"—he claims that some of the reported successes of various torture methods are not fact but actually fantasies of what the torturers themselves can do. You see where I'm going with this, I hope. I mean, even if the results are partly fantastical and not real, though I have evidence to prove otherwise, these made-up stories are still impacting the listeners, initiating fear of the extent of what we're capable of. Hence all this emphasis on cultivating stronger imaginations, stronger modes of storytelling when it comes to our capabilities. Now, let's get back to our reasons for establishing our museum in this unique shape and form, focusing on sound. I should say that the more we studied the history of the profession, the more I realized how justified and indispensable our approach is, today more than ever. Visual documentation works for violent techniques that mutilate and leave marks on the prisoners' bodies, but today, in the tradition of democracies around the world—so smart of them, really, I must admit—we, too, have been increasingly using subtler torture techniques, which are not necessarily brutal in the traditional sense, and as a result, visual documentation will not really accomplish the goal. These days, we mainly use two methods: psychological torture and what Rejali calls "clean torture," in which the techniques are still physical but don't leave marks on the body or, in some cases, tend toward methods that cause internal harm that cannot be seen immediately. So with methods such as these, recording the voice of the tortured works much better, because it allows for a more expansive coverage of the range of our work's impact on the receiver, regardless of the after-torture effects on their bodies. Let me give you a concrete example. You have all probably seen images that are said to be of the torture victims of our close ally, President Bashar al-Assad. Regardless of whether his government was behind the state of these bodies, these images, though important and impressive in a historical, archival sense, are limited in what they deliver to us. Do they show the psychological pressure that was exerted on these people while they were still alive? No. Do they show the real interpersonal dynamic between them and those in power? No. Seeing images of the end result matters, yes, but there is much more to what goes on in the various types of interactions between us and our prisoners, so documenting the process is as important, if not more so—and if we can do it in novel ways, we could increase the impact of the presentation on the audience. Another thing these images from Syria have revealed to us is the hypocrisy of your governments, since in the face of these revelations, they have done nothing to stop or persecute those responsible. So if Mr. Assad's government was the one behind this torture, he has definitely been having a good laugh, patting himself on the back. What other proof is needed for your leaders, who pose as righteous defenders of human rights, who claim they're so different from us, who call themselves the saviors of the world, to act? It's all nothing but a joke. Moreover, if everyone knows who is behind this torture and yet no one is able or willing to do anything about it beyond making empty statements for show, then it really is a shame for their so-called perpetrators not to own their orders and actions. If one believes in what one is doing, why hide? Why not take pride in it? Everything is a matter of perspective. Consider the us's position on this. Just change the rhetoric, call what you're doing something else, pass laws about it, say it's necessary for your national security, and you're good to go. Even if activists and organizations speak out against you, no one can take any meaningful legal action to stop you. This is another reason I believe our museum is revolutionary. First of all, it's not about a distant past but instead an ongoing history we're living in. Second, it's not offered with a sense of shame, or from a position of "let's learn from our mistakes and avoid them in the future," but rather with pride, as an educational center through which we can pass on our knowledge and achievements. In any case, the use of sound as our central medium provides the most intimate methodology that I know of, a peculiar corporeal, living, breathing form of documentation. The other intriguing fact about sound recordings is that the detainees' voices and the sounds they make, of pain or frustration or even joy, come from the depths of their bodies, from inside them, unlike the scars that are on the surface, and as a result, when these sounds reach us, they leave in-depth and oftentimes unconscious marks within us, not easily forgotten or recovered. From yet another angle, in this globalized world, focusing on the sound element makes the museum more portable. It would be easier for it to travel for presentation in other countries, because sound does not have materiality, no physical weight except for the equipment, which we can just borrow on location, while the internal emotional burden it leaves on its audience is heavy, which is exactly what we're looking for. But I should confess that there have been some obstacles and concerns along our path. For example, in recent years, one of our nightmares has been

the rising influence of entities such as Forensic
Architecture and Bellingcat, which use new technologies to expose what they consider human rights violations. One of Forensic Architecture's investigations was
to recreate a blueprint of the Saydnaya Military Prison
in Syria. Our ally Bashar al-Assad has been pretty successful in not letting any images from the prison out, but
Forensic Architecture sat down with a few prisoners
who got out, I'm not sure how, and used their memories
of their time in the prison to map it out. And these
memories were mainly of the sounds they had heard
inside the establishment, because, often stuck in their
individual cells or blindfolded, they hadn't seen much,
but they had heard what went on around them, and that
was what actually helped the Forensic Architecture
researchers do what they called "acoustic modeling."
One of the people invited to that project was a Jordanian
scholar-artist named Lawrence Abu Hamdan, who
works on audio and uses the phrase "earwitness" in his
works to refer to prisoners and any other witnesses who
remember and testify based on what is heard instead of
what is seen, which is what most people immediately
think about when they hear the word "witness." In one
short interview I watched, he talks about how sound
cannot be contained and will always leak, which I don't
agree with, because in this day and age, you can totally
soundproof a space to make sure nothing goes in or out,
not even sound. These people with such amazing levels
of specialization are threats to our professional free-

doms. Let me pull up his website. I want to share something he notes there. "The whispers of inmates became
four times quieter after the 2011 protests began." He
means the Syrians' foolish disruptions of order in their
country. He then continues, "In the absence of any other
material evidence, the nineteen-decibel drop in the
capacity to speak stands as testament to the transforma-
tion of Saydnaya from a prison to a death camp. In these
nineteen decibels we can hear the disappearance of
voice, and the voices of the disappeared." Isn't that last
sentence poetic? Despite their being a nuisance, the way
Abu Hamdan and Forensic Architecture work with
sound is quite interesting to us, and our work is definitely in conversation with theirs, but there are two
main differences. First, they have to use memories and
descriptions of sounds, the prisoners' after-the-fact testimonies, while we have access to actual ongoing sounds
that we can record firsthand. Second, obviously, our
intentions are different too. They are using sounds to
create the prison map, for use in courts of law or for raising awareness through museums and galleries, and as
for us, I think it's clear by now that we're aiming for
something far more striking and exciting. This is all
quite fascinating to me, how we are all interconnected,
and how we are all also inspired by and learning from
the natural world. Have you heard of the creatures in
deep waters that use echolocation as a mechanism for
seeing, literally using sound instead of their eyes, to help
them navigate? Isn't that what we're doing? The inmates

in our cells, the audience here, and even we ourselves, when we do interrogations or audio surveillance, we all rely on the verbal and nonverbal cues offered to us by sound to find our way around. Anyway, some of the sounds the prisoners in Saydnaya reported were simply those of the rain falling, leaves of trees rustling in the wind, objects being moved, or ordinary noises made by guards or their fellow prisoners. This is something our prisoners, too, recount often. They also talk about how they listen for deafening silences, which can be the terrifying signs that their fellow prisoners have fainted or died. Silence is its own sound. It is also mentioned in the book *White Torture,* which was compiled by one of our fiercest enemies and current prisoners, Narges Mohammadi. I am obviously very irritated and angered by her, but part of me also enjoys the constant battle between us. I'm secretly proud that this one enemy giving our system so much trouble is a woman. According to the female prisoners who are quoted in her book, silence became the main sound they listened to when they underwent long periods of solitary confinement. That's why in the recordings offered in the museum, you'll hear, mixed with the sounds of prisoners crying or experiencing pain or babbling unintelligible words, or simply the sounds of the torture instruments at work, stretches of silence, long and short, during which you'll be hearing only the prisoners' breathing, along with ambient sounds from the wind, the cars outside the prison complex, the footsteps in the cells or hallways, the prisoners' bodies moving. The inclusion of silence and ambient sounds is important because they recreate, in the museum, the realistic aura of the atmosphere in the prison and the torture room, which will facilitate the visitors' true-to-life experience. You might also hear, at some moments, instances of laughter. Yes, I can see the surprise on your faces, but this is true. Our work is complicated, and each prisoner or situation demands its own mode of interrogation. So there are instances in which an interrogator tries techniques to build trust and rapport, for example, by telling an anecdote or a joke and making the prisoner laugh. You might resist believing what I'm going to say now, but it's not like our people always consider the prisoners inhuman; it's not uncommon for us to want to genuinely get to know the human being on the other side of the table, to learn how to best speak their language—I mean metaphorically, not that they speak other languages, though that happens too, once in a while. There are also instances of laughter among the officers, or hysterical laughter from the prisoners in solitary confinement: I swear it happens. All in all, for the sake of consistency in our field recordings, we created a system that we've been adhering to throughout our process. For the interrogation and torture sessions, we start recording ten minutes before we start the interrogation and torture session and continue for ten minutes after we wrap up, making sure the recording includes all ambient sounds, especially any unexpected ones. We could have easily eliminated these extra sounds

either by using soundproofing materials in the interrogation and torture rooms or by using sound-editing
software afterward to extract them, but we decided
keeping them would create a more natural effect, which
is more aligned with our goals for recreating the eeriness
of the space and offering our visitors a holistic, embodied experience. Besides Narges Mohammadi and
another similarly resistant female prisoner, Nasrin
Sotoudeh, there are two other political prisoners from
whom I've personally learned a lot. They are Zia Nabavi
and Hesam Salamat. I was once just scrolling through
Instagram, using, of course, a fake account my team set
up, which we all have access to, and I happened upon an
Instagram live broadcast between the two of them. At
least one of them was, at the time, still awaiting his
court ruling, out on bail, so I was quite astonished by
their courage; this was, mind you, not just any chat.
They were talking about solitary confinement and torture in our prisons, discussing it using both their lived
experiences and in-depth philosophical analysis. I took
so many notes during their conversation. One of the
points they brought up was how after losing their social
network outside the prison, what they called their "others," they found some new others inside, including not
only other prisoners but also guards and interrogators. It
was quite nice to hear them acknowledge this particular
relationship built between us. To hear them say they
sometimes wished their interrogator would call them for
a session, because with no external stimulus, the deafen-

ing silence of their cells would become unbearable. Of course, we have long been aware of this, and that's why we often leave the prisoners to themselves for a while, in solitary confinement—some of my colleagues even use the phrase "leave them to rot in their cells"—before we call them in again for further questioning. Either Zia Nabavi or Hesam Salamat then mentioned that some prisoners would even put their fingers into electrical outlets to feel a minimal electrocution, because at least that was some kind of external stimulus, bringing them back to their bodies and making them feel something, anything, which, according to the prisoners, was much better than becoming numb in total isolation, cut off from the world outside and ultimately from oneself. They also discussed that they were aware that we were aware of the significance of their personal objects to them. They pointed out that the removal of objects, such as their glasses, cigarettes, or even their toothbrush, harmed them not just because of the utility of these objects but also because of the prisoners' extra attachment to them, especially in solitary confinement. And they knew that when we gave them back, or offered them, for example, a cigarette during interrogation, they could easily break down and confess simply for the object, or similarly, to get visiting hours with family. They didn't use these terms, but in our vernacular, we categorize these methods as "kind torture" or "sympathy torture." One phrase they did use that stood out to me was "corporeal time" or "bodily time," which I'm trans-lating literally here, so I'm not sure if these are the best English-language equivalents, but the way they explained it was, the body helps us keep our relationship with time, so in solitary confinement, one has to do some form of physical activity, walk around the cell or do push-ups, so that one does not drown completely in one's mind. They also got into differentiating between imagination and illusion: imagination as something still related to and grounded in the reality around you, but illusion as having no contact point with reality. They argued, therefore, that someone in solitary confinement could be ruined by succumbing to illusions, while imagination could actually help them through. So the question that comes up for us is, how to push the prisoners *toward* hallucination and illusions and all the way *away* from imagination. During their three-hour-long Instagram livestream, I experienced a lot of conflicting emotions. To see their minds perform with such exactitude while they continued to carry the wounds we so proudly gave them, physically and psychologically, to see them asking their audience to be more empathetic toward those who are freed and are supposed to come back to normal life, to watch them carry those sorrows but still manage to go beyond them and calmly analyze the situation they lived, deconstructing and thinking through the intricacies of our system and the impact it had on them in such a holistic, emotional, corporeal, and intellectual manner, and for them to courageously share all that with the public, was quite something. For them to be both inside the experience and standing distant enough from it to be able to observe it, I confess, struck me as an exceptional feat that came about as a result of, to use one of the concepts they themselves mentioned, their unique "subjectivity." They did the livestream and the in-depth analysis because, as they put it, they believed in the importance of demystifying what many others might be going through as well . . . I almost burst into tears. I wanted to both shut them up and reach out and embrace them. As someone who has dedicated her life to the world they were exposing, I felt so seen, my powers acknowledged. For a moment, I even thought it would be great to hire them for the museum project, but obviously we couldn't for security reasons. If only my own colleagues could sit so peacefully with the totality of their beings and be able to reflect on it all, imagine where we would be standing today. Frankly, and please don't repeat this elsewhere, I even felt jealous of them. I wished I could take over their whole beings, they were so beautiful and so strong . . . This focus on the prisoners, on the tortured, might, on the surface, be seen as a gesture toward memorializing and honoring those who have been inflicted with pain, which actually works to our benefit, fooling our audience into tagging along, but our real intention is to show the power of our methods and how they impact different individuals differently. We've observed that the outcome of an arrest and imprisonment depends on many variables, such as the prisoner's personal and professional background, the way we invade their homes and offices, the language used with them before and after arrest, how we treat their families and friends outside the prison, as well as the specific conditions of their arrest and imprisonment. Hesam Salamat and Zia Nabavi discussed how our arrests, including theirs, often happen when suspects are at their most vulnerable or weakest—for example, when a parent is sick or in the middle of the night—and how that heavily affected them over the course of their sentences, which I was glad to hear. In a way, the relationship between our work on the ground and our museum project has been a multidirectional one, since each feeds the other and helps us refine our techniques. My hope is that, with our Sound Museum opening, other governments can benefit and take inspiration from our exhibitions, as well as from our education center and archives, which I believe are among the most exhaustive and public in our field, covering not only our own achievements but also what has been done around the world in different eras. Sharing our knowledge with the world will spotlight and validate our rightful status in the field of torture, while indirectly providing our politicians with leverage in diplomatic relations. Another unique aspect of our project—and I want to apologize for taking up so much of your time before the tour, but there's just so much material, and I don't want you to miss anything. I might not be doing the best job organizing it, but I personally prefer this meandering, more organic way of presenting our work to you; it just feels more intimate to me, like a gathering of friends sharing stories rather than a boring bureaucratic presentation, and I promise we'll have a break soon, before heading into the main part of the museum—anyway, another unique aspect of our project is in the facilities and support we have provided for our team, from physical training to mental health services and financial incentives. One of the issues we noticed early on in former prisoners' memoirs or social media posts was the attention they gave to working out as well as trying different techniques to keep themselves mentally healthy, especially if they were in solitary confinement. They describe walking around their cells, doing push-ups, really any kind of movement, to keep themselves in as good a shape, both physically and psychologically, as possible. Our guards have also been seeing this in the cells and the prison courtyards. What surprised us, however, was seeing that many of the former prisoners used their experiences to create guidelines and suggestions for those who might find themselves in similar positions. They try to help families figure out the basic logistics of visits and what items to bring prisoners, or how to psychologically support the prisoners, for example, by reminding them that the world outside has not forgotten them and cares for them, while, on the other hand, continuing to talk of the prisoners any chance they get on their social media or elsewhere to keep them fresh in people's memories so the public does not stop advocating for them, which they believe helps with either easing the prison conditions or their possible release. The psychological burden these former prisoners talk about is something many of my team members and I noticed in ourselves as well. The toll this work has been taking on our team, and consequently our families and loved ones, is huge. I had heard about the innovative work environments that some companies, especially start-ups and tech companies, not just outside of Iran but also here, have been creating to take care of their employees, not merely for the sake of the employees' personal health but also because, according to studies, they benefit their productivity and work ethics and therefore the company as well. So to train our staff and keep them fit, we immediately contracted two gyms close to our offices for our exclusive access, along with some of the best personal trainers in the city, always to be on-site; we didn't mandate participation, since that could have backfired, but we offered all team members free membership and incentives, especially since all of us, as women, have unfortunately grown up with sports not being given priority in our lives—it took me personally several excruciating years of consistent work with an amazing and patient personal trainer to be able to make something of a habit out of it. We have, moreover, brought on board a full-time clergywoman, one of the high-level instructors from the women's Islamic seminary, one who sees the value in our feminist struggles for equity, to accommodate the religious and spiritual needs of our team members, because, according to Rejali, "when torturers act consistently with their moral or religious beliefs, they may escape torture unscathed." On top of that, we have brought along a few full-time mental health professionals to offer our team members private counseling sessions. We thought about doing group sessions as well, but the nature of our work doesn't really allow that. These were separate from and in addition to the psychologists already on our team who are in charge of research, studying our interrogation methods and consulting with us about new techniques. There has historically been a close tie between what we do on the ground and the fields of psychology and philosophy, and one recent example that has now been made public and should be of interest to at least a few of you here involves the two American psychologists at the center of the US developments in the field of torture post-9/11. If you have not seen the movie *The Report*, I highly recommend it, as it is quite suspenseful and entertaining while also being informative. Though it aims to demonstrate that the torture program was misinformed and unsuccessful, it proves how indispensable psychologists are to prison systems. One of the lessons we've learned in this area, I believe it's Rejali who talks about this, either in his book or on the podcast I mentioned, is that the low-level staff who are implementing the torture are more harmed than those in higher-up positions giving the orders. And I swear, we don't want madmen and madwomen working for us. It would often be hard to manage them and order them around, even though many people, as I explained earlier, prefer to believe that's the case here.

As a result of Rejali's insights, we decided to expand our mental health services beyond the museum team and hire more psychologists, counselors, and social workers to care for the torturers and interrogators working in our whole prison system as well. But let me tell you—this proved to be a big challenge, since many of my superiors and colleagues, especially the men, do not believe in psychological care. It took us some time, and many presentations and informative pamphlets, before they were even open to trying such care in a limited capacity, but when they saw how such support translated into results during sessions, they approved a larger budget as well as incentives to encourage our men and women on the ground to take advantage of the offerings. Another thing people believe about us is that only individuals with particular dispositions are made for and can survive doing this kind of job, but this is true only to the extent that one needs certain qualities or interests for any profession; for example, to be a truck driver or a teacher or a detective or a storyteller or a surgeon or a corpse washer. How are we any different? As Rejali points out on the podcast, we are not monsters—as we say in Persian, "We don't have horns," or as you say, "We don't bite" . . . In any case, what he means is that we don't need certain biological dispositions to do what we do. He cites studies and evidence to show that with the right incentives and under the right conditions we all, you all, everyone, has a thirst for and inclination toward violence. If I remember correctly, he says that the lack of clear rules, limits, and meaningful monitoring, and knowing that one is not going to face any legal ramifications for exceeding those that do exist, along with some other conditions, create the perfect environment for people to become violent. So please, spare me your horrified looks and judgmental nods; we are all more or less the same. It's just a matter of whether you are in the position to resist these urges and tendencies, are able to say no. And there are a big enough number of people, not just in our country, but elsewhere too, who go for it. At the archival center, we also offer memoirs from our interrogators and torturers, from different age groups and backgrounds, which cover not just the professional sides of their lives but also the personal and inspirational moments; some of these documents are full-length manuscripts and some are shorter pieces that we have collected in anthologies. This was something we were able to do with little effort and a rather small budget, because many of our colleagues jumped at the opportunity to tell their stories in a situation that was not only free of negative judgment but also actually celebrated their lives, which is quite rare. The impact of these documents is, we believe, pretty far-reaching, as they will ensure visitors, especially of future generations who won't be direct witnesses to our era and will have only these narratives, see us as human beings like themselves. I want to acknowledge that we are not the first ones to do this. I remember some French torturers published their memoirs in the 1990s, and let's include in this category the memoirs of US presidents and defense secretaries and military generals who, even using the faulty standards of international organizations such as the UN, could be labeled as war criminals, men and women whose violence affects not just a few individuals but entire nations—maybe we should call them super-torturers rather than, as they wish to be known, superpowers. But let's move on from memoirs to another type of material in our archives, that is, recordings of the pre-torture voices of the prisoners in interrogation paired with their post-torture voices, so the listener can hear the impact of the process. We're still debating whether to move these snippets to the main wing of the museum or just hold on to them as extra archival material for those who want to study the topic further. We're also debating whether to get consent from our visitors to record their voices, sounds, or silences while they're being exposed to the audio exhibitions in the museum space. It would be interesting to study the way this immersive, creative experience influences them, what they talk to each other about, how long or deep their silences are, or how their breathing changes. We're seriously considering that for phase two of the project, after we receive some general feedback about what we've put together here and, we hope, secure more money for expanding the project. But of course we already have security cameras installed, so the material they capture could be used to do a test run to help make a final decision on that. Let me now return to our architectural design for a moment. You probably did this as a child too. You know when you hold a sea-shell to your ear and hear the sea in it? Wasn't that a magical moment? I remember we had one seashell in our house that was quite big. I learned during our research that the type is called a conch shell, and whenever I felt nervous or anxious, I would pick it up from the shelf and hold it to my ear for a while, and I would imagine myself sitting by a beautiful sea or ocean at sunset. Quite peace-ful. I never knew why exactly the sound was there, just imagined the seashell had naturally recorded the sounds of the waves in its chambers. That's why I suggested, from day one, that our architectural team look into the form of a seashell for our sound center and museum, asking them first to research the cause of the seashell phenomenon. Apparently, there are different hypothe-ses. One that has been disproven is that we are hearing the sound of the waves within it. Another is that it helps us hear the blood circulating in our own ears, which would have been perfect symbolism for us, but unfortu-nately that, too, has been disproven. The real reason is that the seashell acts like a wind instrument whose physical shape causes the air to vibrate more strongly inside and thus amplifies the ambient sounds around it, an explanation that still aligns pretty nicely with our intentions here, as the museum's seashell structure fur-ther echoes and amplifies the audio of the torture along with any other sounds produced in the space. Isn't that amazing? The team also suggested we bring in elements of Persian and Islamic architecture, especially considering that several of our mosques, most prominently the Imam Mosque of Isfahan, a UNESCO World Heritage site, have unique acoustic qualities because of their architectural designs. Without the need for a microphone, they amplify the voices in certain spots of the space or create holy echoes of the calls to prayer. Eventually, our architects collaborated with our museologists and came up with a heavenly and yet practical design that combines the concept of a seashell, though more subtly and abstractly, with elements of our ancient architecture, using old-style bricks, clay, and turquoise tiles and thereby presenting a complex sense of historicity as well modern freedom and flow, allowing for the most imaginative, effective, and user-friendly exhibition format. You probably already noticed our breathtaking design when you entered the establishment, but you'll see it in greater detail once we're inside the main wing. Some of our architects, interior designers, and museologists are here today too, to answer any further questions you might have, so please don't be shy, just jot them down so you don't forget them. Now that I've mentioned my memories of the seashell, some of you might be curious about what my childhood and youth were like, the years before I joined the police force and ultimately the interrogation unit to serve my country. Well, I had a pretty regular childhood, but there were two particular events that made me realize what power I could have when I grew up, if I joined the police force. Of course, in the beginning, I didn't have a clear vision of what role or position I could serve in, but I was so fascinated by the power the police held over the public: I mean, not just the police, but the various forms of them, such as the paramilitary, the militia, the Basij, the Komiteh, which existed during my childhood but doesn't anymore, the special forces, the morality police—any of them, really. The first event which I vividly remember to this day is from my elementary school years, so perhaps I was eight or nine years old. Some of the details aren't so clear anymore, but the feeling of that day is so alive, it's as if I experienced it just a moment ago. One morning I was headed to school in someone's car—I don't remember whether it was a taxi, or a friend's parent's car, or what, and I don't remember who I was with—and when we arrived at the square near our school, there was a huge crowd, and all the roads were blocked by police forces, which was unusual that early in the morning. So there we were, stuck in traffic, behind a mass of people, with no way to go backward or forward, and I think the adult we were with said something about not looking, which actually had the reverse impact and made us, the kids, more curious, so I looked up and ahead and saw, in the middle of the square, a few cranes mounted on trucks. It took me a moment to notice that there were things dangling from them. I didn't realize then what they were, but I was awestruck by the whole thing; it was as if they had put a movie on pause: everyone gathering there was silent; there was a sense of shock in the air. Anyway, we waited until everything cleared out and the dangling things were brought down. I didn't see what happened to them after; the cranes drove away, and the people dispersed. When we arrived at school, I remember there was such chaos. Our headmistress and our teachers were all at the entrance or in the hallways, running around or standing still in shock, and the kids were crying, and the staff started calling parents to come in, and I don't know how much time passed like that, but I remember my mother standing by my side at the door at some point, or maybe she was in the car from the very beginning, maybe she was taking me to school, but I remember the hassle and the crying and the confusion and the helplessness in the eyes of the adults, and I'm not sure when I overheard that the things hanging in midair were actually human bodies with their heads covered in black cloth, their hands tied behind their backs. Executed. The adults were whispering that the men were drug traffickers. I'm not sure how many they were, maybe two or three. Anyhow, those scenes never really left me, and I still can't fully describe how I felt while we all waited there and I watched the powerlessness of the adults, paralyzed in the face of what was happening. Growing up, I kept thinking about the magical power of that spectacle, all those people brought to a silent standstill. And mind you, I believe it was not just fear in the air but also fascination and some kind of excitement. While we're on the subject, I want to add here that during my career I've witnessed several other scenes of public hanging in which the audience was not standing still in silence but rather moved around quite a bit, even cheered and clapped for the executioners. So either I misremember that childhood event, or people react differently depending on the occasion, or over the years their behavior has changed. Either way, the point is, it's quite amazing how one event can have such an in-depth, long-term impact on a child. Another event I haven't been able to forget didn't actually happen to me but was something I heard one of my classmates recount while we were sitting in my university's all-female cafeteria. We were sharing memories from our elementary school day trips. Many girls were telling stories about going to museums or parks, but one girl, I remember she was pretty tall and had a strong build, started telling us about being taken to the city's main cemetery. We were all kind of surprised and thought she was joking, but her face got very serious as she looked around and lowered her voice before she continued on. She told us the ride to the cemetery had been fun, all of them sharing their snacks, people watching, playing, not paying attention to the religious studies teacher who was trying to give them some kind of sermon. She wasn't sure why their parents had signed the permission slip for them to go on that particular day trip but guessed that maybe they hadn't been told where the kids were being taken. Anyway, they arrived in Behesht-e Zahra, and the bus took them to the area with the newer plots, and that's where they were told to get off. In the not so far-off distance was a funeral, with the family and friends of the deceased gathered around, and while the body was being lowered into the grave by two men and a cleric recited prayers over the loudspeaker, the religious studies teacher talked to the kids about death and the afterlife. Then she asked them to turn away from the funeral and gather around a newly dug grave that was perhaps awaiting the arrival of its new resident. The teacher began to explain Islamic burial rituals to them and then suddenly asked the girl, the one telling the story, to jump into the grave and lie there, to pretend to be dead. The girl stood there in shock for a few seconds, staring into the void of the grave, before beginning to plead with her teacher to spare her the mission, but the more she begged, the less leniency the teacher showed, reprimanding her for her fear. In the end, while all the kids were dead silent, the girl had gone down into the grave and lain there while the teacher continued with her detailed lesson on human mortality and the importance of living by Islamic moral codes. As my classmate recounted the memory all those years later, her hands trembled around her disposable teacup, and I could see fear and hatred rising up in her eyes. I'm not sure if what she described was true or if she was just trying to intimidate us, but even if it was the latter, it showed me, maybe for the first time, in a very concrete way, the impact of death, even mere proximity to it, on kids. More recently, I saw a video on someone's Twitter of a little girl named Sharmin playing with her dolls, using different objects to create a structure resembling a prison cell. She was first putting the dolls in the cell and then setting them free from it, calling out to her mother to come celebrate this freedom with her. It seemed that her father was a political activist who had been taken to prison. Psychology books discuss how malleable kids' psyches are, but it was quite thrilling to actually see a real-life case revealing our influence on the younger generation. We also saw, during the most recent upheavals as well as several previous ones, how comprehensively our younger generation can be manipulated into serving as mouthpieces for our enemies, even lose their lives for values that have no place in our ideal society. That's why one of our procedures after arrests of minors has been to send them to special psychiatric and juvenile detention centers, where we can, under highly controlled conditions, away from the impure effects of the internet, their friends, and their parents, evaluate and reeducate them, bring them to their senses, and ensure that they're on the right path to serve our larger sociopolitical structures rather than following their own frivolous, selfish interests or those of our international enemies. That's also why our museum is offering special tours and discounts for students and those in younger age groups, and we hope to begin them at the start of the new school year. You know, the human psyche never ceases to amaze me, so reshaping the young psyches so they better align with our own desires has been one of our key priorities. Let me tell you about a dream I had in the early phases of our project. I was in a room, and one of my male colleagues, a higher-ranking officer, was standing by an alcove or closet in which several long, black raincoats were hanging. He kept sliding them one by one to the far-right side of the alcove, and it was as if the alcove and raincoats were endless. I was watching all this from the left corner of the room. There were a few other colleagues in the room as well, all in uniform. The officer suddenly turned around to face us while the raincoats continued moving on their own, and I noticed that he had a gun in his right hand. At first, I thought he was aiming at the guys in the middle of the room, but he unexpectedly turned and targeted me. I froze, in shock, for what seemed like eternity. He kept staring at me, and when I heard a shot, at first I thought I was hit, but then I noticed he had aimed at a male colleague to my right. When I looked at the colleague, he was touching his forehead, where the bullet had entered his skull. He kept blinking but seemed very relaxed. The bullet hole gradually became a congealed red dot, as if made of wax, and all of a sudden, all the men started screaming and ran out of the room. That's when I heard some voices in my bedroom—I mean my real bedroom, not in the world of the dream—and I woke up, startled. I then noticed these weird creatures in my room, part human and part animal, dancing around my bed, but when they saw that I had woken up, they started running toward the door, the same way the men in my dream had. Before leaving the room, one of them paused and placed a large bag on the floor by the door. Everything felt so real that I half got up from my bed and leaned in that direction to see what they'd left behind for me. I was very surprised when I didn't find anything there and kept waiting for the creatures to come back, hoping they would, not sure what I thought they would reveal to me, and I couldn't sleep for many hours after that. I was terrified of what the officer in my dream had done, because I knew that he and the guy he shot were buddies in real life, and I also felt saddened by the creatures leaving me all alone in my bedroom. In the morning, the first thing I did was call my spiritual advisor to recount to her the events of the night. She said she would bless an amulet and write out a special prayer for me, both of which I could pick up later that day. She instructed me to read the prayer every night for forty consecutive nights, and after that, to read it every Thursday night before going to bed. She explained that the creatures were djinns who were celebrating my life being spared in the dream, and the bag they had left me was full of the resources I needed for the completion of the museum, and even though I hadn't literally picked it up, it had been successfully and symbolically delivered to me because I had seen it clearly and acknowledged it. She also advised me to be wary of the higher-ranking officers, who would probably become envious of the development of my project and might attempt different strategies to hinder its completion. Wait . . . Why was I sharing my dream with you? Oh, I was speaking about our psyches, their strange, still unknowable relationships to our past, present, and future reality. Anyway . . . Going back to our plans for the museum, one thing I want to highlight again is the significance of what we've recorded in our archive and education center for posterity. We want to make sure we have everything documented correctly so it's all ready to be presented according to our wishes if ever our government isn't here anymore. I know this might sound surprising coming from me, and it's probably something I shouldn't be saying out loud, to you of all people, and God forbid it happens any time soon, but if we have rightly learned history's lesson, we know that sooner or later our time will be up, particularly in this region of the so-called Middle East, a very problematic directional designation with Western orientation, but I won't get into that now. I'm going to say something now that you can't, I mean, you won't be allowed to, repeat outside this space . . . I personally am going to make sure about that beyond our agreements with your editors. To be honest, I've been a bit concerned about the signs of decline in the supremacy of our leadership the past few years, with the widespread protests, for example, which we did clamp down on, but still, there are the internal conflicts that keep popping up in various sectors of our government and some recent international blowbacks that have diminished our power on the global geopolitical scene. So I'm very glad I started this project when I did, to make sure we complete at least the preliminary phases. Even if I'm wrong about these signs, and I truly hope I am, even if we continue our mighty reign for years to come, death will eventually and unfortunately befall us, each and every one of its servants, and the younger generation won't have direct access to our insights, nor will they necessarily profess the exact same ideals as ours. That's why I believe in the urgency of my task at this moment in time. We need to have our narrative orchestrated and ready for use the way we desire it to be used. This will give us some control over how our story is going to be told, and how we'll be remembered. Pretty smart, right? Along these lines, our work at the center is also important as it relates to the possibility of our deeds one day being brought to the so-called courts of justice and international tribunals, or to people's tribunals which are judicial gestures organized by society members and have no real legal ramifications. Do you know about them? There was a recent international people's tribunal held in London that evaluated some of the security measures we had to take in Iran in 2019, and after much fuss, they came up with verdicts saying we were responsible for this and that, but as I said, these don't translate into any legal actions against us, so there you go. Anyway, after that one, I became curious about these so-called people's tribunals and started to do some research on them. Apparently the first one, called the Russell Tribunal, was organized by Bertrand Russell and hosted by Jean-Paul Sartre, along with several other philosophers and writers, including Simone de Beauvoir, whose book *The Second Sex* has been illuminating for me, despite my finding some of it quite problematic. That first tribunal, held in 1966, was aimed at investigating the US foreign policy and military presence in Vietnam, but the nice thing about it was it didn't change anything about the actions the US was taking around the world, and I don't believe the rulings were even acknowledged by the US government. So yes, there have been snags with legal courts as well as these symbolic ones, but most of them, as I know and you know too, in your hearts, even if you don't want to admit it, are just decorative and don't really have any practical impact. Even if they make one or two parties pay for what they did, they don't stir up meaningful fear or act as deterrents for future generations coming to power. Let me tell you, when one looks at historical accounts of these courts, or even broadcasts of the contemporary ones, one can also not help but question the accuracy of the testimonies against various systems of power, and that's true not just with regard to these courts but throughout history in general—we'll never know how much fiction is mixed up with the truth, and this mixing might not even be intentional or malicious but just a function of human memory. Arendt, in her book on Eichmann, touches on this issue and questions the accuracy of some of the testimonies against him, wondering how much was truly in accordance with what was experienced personally by witnesses and how much stemmed from indirect memories, what people had read or heard, their having made others' memories their own, or even imagined memories from scratch. And if I remember correctly, she even goes on to call one of the testimonies "propaganda" and also points to some people's righteous concerns about whether the Zionist regime, though of course she doesn't use the term "Zionist," was even "suitable"—and that's her exact word—to be in charge of the proceedings for Eichmann, since they couldn't really be impartial throughout the process. You see, when, if, it comes to being judged, either by official courts or the courts of public opinion, things quickly become very complicated, so we have many good reasons to document things, provide our own evidence, and curate witness narratives properly, as we see fit. Anyway, let's move on to some of the advanced uses of technology in our museum, and I promise we'll soon start the tour. I'm sure when you hear about this one cutting-edge technology, you'll agree that it's just amazing. So we've been using a livestream system: the visitor can choose to either sit in a private room, put on headphones, and listen individually to the sounds coming from a cell, or experience these sounds with other people in a room where they are broadcast through a high-quality surround sound system. The cells used for the livestream were handpicked through a process of elimination. We started with a larger pool, and then, over time, we noticed that specific cells had better acoustic qualities. Then, to maximize the quality of our output, we arranged for the inmates kept in those spaces to be the ones whose voices we're most interested in. For example, some prisoners sing, some begin to talk to themselves after a while, some are prone to making sounds in reaction to any movement or sound outside their cell. Note that we are not interested in group rooms or public areas of the wards, where conversations are also happening, but rather spaces in which the individual is completely alone. We also offer our visitors the option to experience surprise livestreams, for which we rotate between various cells to keep things interesting, especially for those returning. Another project we're hoping to start in the later phases of our endeavor is a collaboration with the music, science, and technology department at Stanford University, to enable our visitors to listen to the recorded voices presented here not only with the acoustics of the cells but also with those of different locations around the country and the world. You might have heard about this project, but I'll just say a bit more, for those of you who have not. Stanford researchers have succeeded in modeling the way audio would sound at different sites. I learned about this in an interview with yet another exiled Iranian scholar, one of our enemies, on the occasion of the passing of Mohammad-Reza Shajarian, the late maestro of traditional Persian music, whose voice was banned here, a decision I never agreed with, just to be clear, because it simply made him more popular, raising him to the ranks of a hero in the eyes of the people. In that interview, they played a recording of his voice as if he were singing in Turkey's Ayasofya, which, if I've got this right, you call Hagia Sophia in English. It gave me chills. I highly recommend it. It was just a few short minutes, but oh my, it was so heavenly, so sacred. Apparently, the building has very unique acoustic qualities, and that was why Shajarian chose it for the experiment, though I feel betrayed because he didn't decide to test his voice at one of our own many cultural heritage sites, or at one of the extravagant mosques we've built in the past few decades. So one of our future hopes is to give our visitors the option of browsing through a list of locations across the globe and picking where they want to hear the sounds made by someone being tortured. This will also spread our enterprise imaginatively beyond our prisons' walls, all over Iran and possibly the world, as if we were omnipresent, had overtaken all these spots and were using them as torture sites. Wouldn't that be an incredible experiment? The key factor at our museum is to ensure that our visitors are not simply listening in passing or while multitasking. That's why we ask everyone to leave their phones, a major source of distraction, behind at the reception desk before they enter the exhibitions wing. To maximize engagement, for some of our displays we also offer and highly encourage the use of blindfolds. We want to invite you to put your whole heart and soul into this journey, imagine that you are in the same space with the prisoner, imagine that you, like them, are stuck inside the prison, imagine that all that is causing these sounds in their bodies and minds is happening within you as well. Also, to make sure that this is a fully embodied experience, we've come up with some engaging, interactive games for you. I don't want to ruin the whole surprise, but I can share a few examples. One of our offerings is our special virtual reality game, which takes you into our cells, solitary confinements, and interrogation rooms, all designed quite closely to what we have in reality without compromising security measures. The game invites you to immerse yourself in our prison system, having the choice to pick who you want to be, from the prisoner to the torturer to all the roles that come in between. Another offering of ours is to give visitors the chance to give orders to a torturer on the ground, through telecom, telling them what to do next with a prisoner, and once they do, you'll hear the results. And I'll tell you about one more: we're also going to give you, at the end of the tour, some sounds as prompts, and we'll ask you to translate them into other forms of art, such as drawings or performances. Our hope is that, in the near future, we can have special tours for artists—invite sculptors to make full-body statues of whom they imagine the sounds came from, writers to come up with fictional accounts of these episodes in the lives of the prisoners, and sound artists and musicians to translate these human voices into other types of soundscapes. In other words, we are curious to see how the emotional and psychological effects of these sounds can . . . what's the word . . . *percolate* through the work of artists. Seeing sound's impact on their imaginations will further allow us to devise more complex methodologies for interrogation and torture, especially of artists, if the need arises at some point. But for now, as I said at the very beginning of my talk, you are the first lucky group to be invited for a private tour of the museum. Up to this point, only a few of our own high-level officials have visited, just a few days ago, to bless the project with their prayers and presence. Following your tour, we will have a period of limited, invitation-only openings, for both our fellow officials and some trusted international figures, before we go fully public. As you might have noticed, not all of you are journalists working in the fields of policing, military, security, or foreign affairs with a focus on Iran, but trust me, each and every one of you is here for a good reason. For example, those of you who cover medicine are here because of your intimate relationship with the human body and mind, which are of course at the center of torture and its success, and those of you who cover music are here to witness our acoustic achievements and tell us what you think about our spatial and sonic experiences, and so on and so forth. So please feel free to offer your feedback about the center as well as our inaugural presentation today. After my talk, you'll have a guided tour, and at the end, you'll be given a tablet on which to fill out an anonymous visitor survey. If you think of any other interactive activities or have suggestions for additional uses of the material in the museum or the archive, or if you simply wish to comment on our offerings and hospitality during today's event—anything you like—please don't hesitate to share. For example, if we decide to study people during their visits, do you think it would work to have them wear some kind of wiring to record their physical reactions or brain waves in response to the different sounds? Or would doing a survey after each visit give us more legible and easily accessible results? Or for those of you in the field of psychology, could you share with us whether, for example, the prisoners' sounds in any way reveal the psychological effects of different torture methods, or whether we can predict the possible traumatic impact of the visit and the sounds on the visitors? Those of you in digital media, we want to hear your ideas about other modes of presentation and how best to use our technological capabilities. Our team of researchers and scholars is, as I've noted, pretty diverse professionally, but you can never have too much input, especially since we're well aware that after working together as a tight team in secrecy for so long, we might have some blind spots—there's no doubt that we will benefit from some outsiders' views and feedback. So we welcome your honest observations and any suggestions you have in the post-tour survey, or if you prefer to talk privately with one of our staff rather than fill out the form, let us know, and we can definitely accommodate that as well. I see one of you raising your hand. Please let me finish and hold on to your question. I promise you'll be given ample time to ask questions after my presentation. We appreciate your investment and interest in the project and want to acknowledge your invaluable role in, God willing, properly introducing us to the world. I know I shouldn't have shared some of what I shared with you today, but I'm in such a celebratory mood, as it's our opening day. I also know that you're not going to publish anything without obtaining our approval first, per the agreements we made with your editors in chief before we secured your visas, made travel arrangements, and offered this exclusive, in-depth story. Whatever you've heard or hear today, you need to use your good judgment, ask yourselves questions such as, "Will this piece keep my family and me safe?" or "Who will my piece serve?" and so on before you decide to include anything in your report on our extraordinary achievement. And we will of course be the ones giving the green light before anything goes to press. I just feel it's necessary, here at the end of my speech, to remind everyone once again that the aim of our project has not been to study whether torture is effective. No, that has never been our question or concern. We already know it's effective. From getting confessions, to deterring people from committing certain acts, to cementing our authority, causing ripple effects across society, the impacts know no bounds. With that in mind, our aim is to reconsider and expand the definition of that effectiveness. This effectiveness is absolutely a result of our most dedicated officers putting their hearts and souls into the work, of their faith in their roles in building a better, more secure future in which everyone can ultimately see the glory of our system of governance. It is inevitable that on this path some lives are sacrificed. No victories in the history of civilization have materialized without some losing their lives. So I'm always very surprised that some onlookers still have a hard time understanding the necessity of sacrifice, of paying a price for our ultimate dreams: building an ideal nation and maintaining the sanctity of our state. Keeping these intentions in mind, my team has done their absolute best to build an innovative, honest, and embodied museum as well as an immersive archive that teaches by example and is descriptive rather than prescriptive. We are not claiming that if an interrogator or torturer does such and such an action in such and such a situation that it will give them certain results, because our work with the human body and psyche is too complex to be completely formulaic. Rather, we offer enough information for our younger officers to watch, hear, and feel what has been going on in our interrogation rooms, so each of them, according to their personal attitudes and the demands of their case, can pick and choose what they find useful. This methodology, more akin to teaching arts rather than hard sciences, will allow us to redefine the study of our field in the larger academic and scholarly arena and reconfigure the direction this knowledge is flowing, not just from scholars toward us but also from us to scholars. It will actually position us as the new scholars crafting the torture discourse, and we will also be able to proudly export our expertise to other governments and step into our rightful place on the global stage. There are so many benefits to this practice of transparency that I sometimes wonder how all these years we have prioritized the benefits of secrecy. To be honest, especially in our day and age, with new technologies and social media platforms sprouting up left and right, secrecy is never complete or ideal. There's always someone somewhere in our own system who reveals something for one reason or another, from showing off to acting out according to some rivalry to working toward the illusion of serving a greater good; and even if none of that happens, we are always unfortunately in the grip of hackers, which is a story in itself. And in this environment, the question of torture's benefits is like the elephant in the room: everyone is aware of it, but no one is willing to talk about it. Maybe people in academia do, sure, but outside the ivory tower, things are still kept largely hush-hush. We should stand up for our achievements rather than fear the limiting morals and laws the international community is holding us accountable to, morals and laws they themselves have found their own smart ways to breach. There's nothing anyone can do to stop us, or I should say, nothing anyone's willing to do. Are they going to go to war against us? Are they going to come for us? Well, they can, but we will just fight them back. So honestly, why should we play our game by their rules? Enough is enough. We are our own sovereign state. We need to be independent and decide what is best for us, what will ensure the continued glories of our nation. Now, before we wrap up, my staff here is going to come around and offer you each a wristwatch, which we kindly ask that you put on right now so when we start the tour, it can record your breathing patterns as well as your heart rate. We're using this tour to pilot this technology before we consider it for the public. The watches allow us to record the depth of the visit's somatic impact. My colleagues are also going to pass around a consent form in a moment, which you must sign before entering the museum, and as you'll see on the form, the data collected here will be used only for furthering our research in the field. We will not sell it to third parties or use it for other commercial purposes, unlike the various companies behind the watches many of you wear of your own will these days. Let's move on now so I can personally accompany you during at least part of the tour before I jump into some other meetings;

I'd like to show you a few of our exhibits myself. I know "show" seems like an odd word to choose when it comes to exhibits of sound, but I've noticed that sound artists actually do use this term. I truly hope that you, our esteemed international journalists, find this private tour of value for yourselves and your media outlets, and remember, this is a rare opportunity you're receiving as a result of your interest in human rights, which is a highly controversial concept manipulated in the hands of Western governments and international institutions, like many other concepts that might have been developed in good faith but are now just one more tool in the hands of imperialist capitalism and neoliberalism. I am well informed on this subject, having spent some years in the US for my graduate studies and then returning home to help and defend the security of our borders, which are constantly under international threat, and thus serve our ideals and our people. I'm aware that the very people I'm referring to might be questioning our sacrifices now, interpreting them otherwise, but history will one day attest to our services to our nation. Now, having nearly reached the end of my talk, I also want to apologize for the long wait for your clearances, but you know that, especially when it comes to this kind of thing, we can't risk any security breaches. We also needed to make sure you were the right first-ever outside audience to share in this glorious experience of sound art. Let me share one last theory about sound before we wrap up. I know, I know, you can tell by now how much I love theory.

Scholar Pedro J. S. Vieira de Oliveira, a Brazilian sound studies researcher, in an essay about disaster and decolonizing sound art, underlines—actually, let me bring up the quotes on the slides, because I remember I added some the other day to the pile. The essay is from this amazing resource *The Bloomsbury Handbook of Sound Art*. He underlines that sound and listening are political as well as "embodied, lived" realities, not just belonging to the "realm of mindful abstraction," and he adds that "situating sound art practice and experience makes explicit that *who* listens matters, and that the listening act is simultaneously informed and co-constituted by the embodied realities of the listener," along with "the materiality of the sonic work." Also: "Listening experiences are as much about the listener as they are about how sounds reveal themselves in the space. They are about . . . the negotiation between their lived materiality—or the political conditions in which they exist or were taken from—and the listener's own." As you see, besides our national security, we also couldn't risk jeopardizing our aesthetic aspirations, so we had to make sure you were the right type of listeners for this first official tour, especially since we are also interested in your feedback, including on the best marketing and publicity measures for promoting the fruits of our labor on an international scale. We are aware of the power of journalists and are grateful for your presence here, and for your forthcoming coverage of our museum in your relatively independent media, and I want to emphasize "relatively" here because we know—and so do you, being intelligent thinkers and writers—that the money that funds your institutions has an effect on the policies set by your editors in chief, even if as individuals you don't necessarily work on a day-to-day basis to promote the agendas that money sets. My team and I are really looking forward to reading what you produce. Finally, one other point I wanted to stress before I finish: our Sound Museum is the result of all the above collective actions and yearslong intersectional collaborations; none of us as individuals would have been able to bring this innovative project to life, so please, a round of applause for everyone on my team who is present here today, and also for those who are either running around behind the scenes to make this as beautiful an opening reception as possible or who were unable to make it for one reason or another. All right, before you enter the exhibition space, I want to invite you to keep yourselves open to what another sound artist, Pauline Oliveros, calls "the whole of the space/time continuum of perceptible sound" and to enter our museum the way she approaches sound, with "no preconceived ideas." To prepare you for what she calls "deep listening," one of my team members will guide you through a few breathing exercises as well as a little specific energy and body work, followed by a short meditation, all designed to open you up to a more expansive range of sounds and affects, to enable each one of you to create your own unique, holistic relationship to the experience we will provide. Last but not least, I want to be sure to give a content warning before the official tour begins. I know you've been listening to me talk for a while now about our field and the creative, practical, and theoretical frameworks and complexities of this project that has been so many years in the making, and I know that many of you are seasoned journalists and have been widely exposed to such topics both domestically and internationally in various drastic situations, but I assure you, what you are about to experience is on a completely different level, and my well-trained team has advised me that it would be wise for me to warn you of this one last time. I am certain that none of you, with all your credentials and your professional dedication, are going to back out at this point. How could you not want to be one of the first beyond our inner circle to gain access to this site, which up until now has been kept completely hidden, and have the rare opportunity to cover it? We just want you to know that we care about your well-being and that you have the choice to opt out if you decide that's best for you, for personal reasons or whatever. We would simply need you to fill out an official form explaining why exactly you're no longer interested, sign a nondisclosure agreement, and write down everything you remember from our time together so far. If any of you are considering that choice, please go ahead and talk to one of my assistants; they're standing right over there. Now, before we lead you into the exhibitions wing, we thought it might be best for you all to take a quick break, use the bathroom if you need to, freshen up, call a loved one or say a prayer or perhaps, if you'd prefer, do your own individual meditation, to warm your hearts and quiet your minds before you immerse yourselves completely in this once-in-a-lifetime corporeal and spiritual experience. My team has also put together a buffet of Persian finger food in the room to your right, brought to you by some of our best chefs in town, who've been revolutionizing the presentation of our superb, delicious traditional cuisine. I'm also going to excuse myself for a few minutes, so I can freshen up and finalize a few things with our tour guides, who are waiting for you on the other side of this door. Meanwhile, please feel free to mingle and relax and enjoy the food, and I'll be back with you in a bit. Please, go ahead. And if you have any questions at this time, you can address them to my assistants, who will be more than happy to help you. Thank you all for being here, and I hope you do enjoy your tour of my Sound Museum.

Coffee House Press began as a small letterpress operation in 1972 and has grown into an internationally renowned nonprofit publisher of literary fiction, essay, poetry, and other work that doesn't fit neatly into genre categories.

Coffee House is both a publisher and an arts organization. Through our *Books in Action* program and publications, we've become interdisciplinary collaborators and incubators for new work and audience experiences. Our vision for the future is one where a publisher is a catalyst and connector.

LITERATURE
is not the same thing as
PUBLISHING

# Funder Acknowledgments

Coffee House Press is an internationally renowned independent book publisher and arts nonprofit based in Minneapolis, MN; through its literary publications and Books in Action program, Coffee House acts as a catalyst and connector—between authors and readers, ideas and resources, creativity and community, inspiration and action.

Coffee House Press books are made possible through the generous support of grants and donations from corporations, state and federal grant programs, family foundations, and the many individuals who believe in the transformational power of literature. This activity is made possible by the voters of Minnesota through a Minnesota State Arts Board Operating Support grant, thanks to the legislative appropriation from the Arts and Cultural Heritage Fund. Coffee House also receives major operating support from the Amazon Literary Partnership, Jerome Foundation, Literary Arts Emergency Fund, McKnight Foundation, and the National Endowment for the Arts (NEA). To find out more about how NEA grants impact individuals and communities, visit www.arts.gov.

Coffee House Press receives additional support from Bookmobile; the Buckley Charitable Fund; Dorsey & Whitney LLP; the Schwab Charitable Fund; and the U.S. Bank Foundation.

## The Publisher's Circle of Coffee House Press

Publisher's Circle members make significant contributions to Coffee House Press's annual giving campaign. Understanding that a strong financial base is necessary for the press to meet the challenges and opportunities that arise each year, this group plays a crucial part in the success of Coffee House's mission.

Recent Publisher's Circle members include many anonymous donors, Patricia A. Beithon, Theodore Cornwell, Jane Dalrymple-Hollo, Mary Ebert & Paul Stembler, Randy Hartten & Ron Lotz, Amy L. Hubbard & Geoffrey J. Kehoe Fund of the St. Paul & Minnesota Foundation, Hyde Family Charitable Fund, Cinda Kornblum, Gillian McCain, Mary & Malcolm McDermid, Vance Opperman, Mr. Pancks' Fund in memory of Graham Kimpton, Robin Preble, Steve Smith, and Paul Thissen.

For more information about the Publisher's Circle and other ways to support Coffee House Press books, authors, and activities, please visit www.coffeehousepress.org/pages/support-coffee-house or contact us at info@coffeehousepress.org.

**poupeh missaghi** is a writer, editor, translator (between English and Persian), and educator. Her debut novel *trans(re)lating house one* was published in 2020 (Coffee House Press). Her translations include *I'll Be Strong for You* by Nasim Marashi (Astra House, 2021) and *In the Streets of Tehran* by Nila (Ithaka Press, 2023).

*Sound Museum* was based on a design by
Bookmobile Design & Digital Publisher Services.
Text is set in Adobe Caslon Pro.